Crave for Pleasure

Complete 10 Part Interracial Erotica Series

ERIC RESHER

Crave For Pleasure/ Eric Resher. -- 1st ed.
Xplicit Press, an imprint of TLM Media LLC

ISBN-13: 978-1-62327-581-5
ISBN-10: 1-62327-581-4
eISBN: 978-1-62327-631-7

Printed in the United States of America

CONTENTS

1 BRANDY'S HOOKUP

Brandy Tuey wrenched her right hand from her sopping cunt hole and tried to suppress multiple orgasms rushing through her hot, eighteen-year-old body. She smoothed her crewneck pink tee down her 30B-27-35 form. She pulled up her jean pants, struggling around the waist, until she remembered to yank her purple thong, with the wedding cake on the front, into place. Buck Henderson, the thirty-year-old black Management Consultant that Brandy babysat for would be home in thirty minutes. He always arrived home at six-thirty in the afternoon, on the dot. Brandy picked up the pink towel off the four-seat leather brown couch, and hurried into their plush bathroom to wash it. It wouldn't dry by the time Buck got home, but he was calm, laid back man. Not at all like her mom told her all black men behaved. Brandy hopped back on the luxury brown couch, tossed her book bag on one end, and wiggled her Nanny 101 book out. She started reading her next day's assignment. She wondered how long it took a sex flush to disappear from an alabaster-white-girl's skin. Damn, she had never timed it.

Brandy's short, straight, ash-blonde hair lay behind both ears and almost reached her neck. It did reach her neck, if she was reclining, as she had been when fantasizing about fucking black Buck, her employer. She imagined him laying her down on the bed and parting her legs. He'd drive his strong, hard dick deep inside her drenched cunt. The beautiful, muscular man played basketball and racquetball to stay in shape. Brandy's smooth, white hands slid over her beautiful feminine neck, hallowed right where a man's Adam apple might bob up and down. Although Brandy considered her round face her greatest asset, her tiny, happy blue eyes cast a playful mood inviting a male to come closer, too. Her eyes even displayed friendliness to any female.

In fact, Brandy's small lips gave the impression she couldn't suck a big black cock. However, Brandy thought she could; she just never had the chance, yet.

Brandy Tuey came from poor parents. They lived at the far end of a trailer park. Some called her white trash, but Brandy carried herself well and dressed neat. Her dad ran off long ago. She worked her way out of the situation by gaining a scholarship to nursing school. Long ago, being a nun caught her curiosity. But, since nuns don't have sex and Brandy always loved to care for others, she settled for being either a nanny, or a nurse. She always loved children, but had a terrible mom. Her Mom called her names and accused her of doing some terrible deeds with black boys who lived on the far end of town, before the trailer park began.

Brandy never did any such thing with those black boys. Nevertheless, they kept glancing their eyes her way in school. She couldn't stop thinking of what sensations and feelings a pair of dark, black hands on her spherical pink, white breasts and tiny, pink nipples might bring. "You'll never amount to anything. You're only worth what is between your legs! You'll never get married!" Well, Brandy stopped listening to her Mom after age fourteen. Fourteen years were terrible, and enough time to

3

realize her Mom's prejudice. Plus, she didn't want to admit that she wanted some black cock, too. Often, when masturbating, Brandy wondered if her mom already had some black dick. Her Mom knew so much about it. Brandy fought through her Mom's mean thoughts to get to the juicy parts of the black men she never slept with and wished she had.

Things may have remained that way; vacant, locked in the dream world of imagination. But when Brandy got to the University, she found her nursing/nanny scholarship only went so far. Her scholarship paid for her dorm room and tuition. She needed to make some extra funds. Fortunately, the University turned out to be near an exclusive, rich neighborhood, where people could afford to pay $10 an hour to a babysitter. When she first applied for the Henderson job, she didn't expect the parents to be dark as the night when the moon was new, but fate was fate. Buck Henderson told her the hours, how much cooking she might do for five-year-old Tawnequa, their daughter, who was in preschool already. She would be needed to watch their daughter after preschool let out, until when they got home from work, which was about two or three hours a day, Monday through Friday.

Buck and his wife, Joycelynn, seemed like a marriage on the rocks. Brandy realized not everyone divorced, or separated, like her parents. The Hendersons worked good jobs. Their house had a living room and, to the left, a huge bedroom. Down the hall was Tawnequa's bedroom and two twin beds separated by a half wall. Their full kitchen, with burlap weave stools around a black and white dotted granite top, went to the right of the living room. A small patio led from the kitchen to a near regulation size pool out back, to do laps. Brandy enjoyed the elegance of their full-sized bathroom and almost blushed when she saw the powder room. The Henderson's didn't have to fight over money and stuff like her parents did. Brandy only knew Joycelynn always seemed to get home after she was gone. This made her curious, though.

Driving home, Brandy needed to touch herself, using her left hand, while keeping her right hand steady on the wheel. She thought several times, "Buck likes me. I have seen him occasionally, on rare occasions, looking me up and down my body. He seemed to stare at my gym shoes all the time. What is that about?" Maybe she could fuck Buck. No! It's just wrong to fuck a married man. If he were free, though? Brandy always went to bed at night thinking that. What if black, muscular Buck divorced his wife? What if, better still, Buck liked to get his hands on her alabaster skin? What if he wanted to push his hard, stiff, black cock between her legs and do naughty other things?

Brandy picked up Tawnequa and arrived at the Henderson's place. She read schoolbooks to the smart, five-year-old dark skinned girl. They'd play with girl Lego blocks and then it was time for her nap, before her parents came home from work at six-thirty in the afternoon. Tawnequa slept as quiet as her black Barbie doll.

Brandy tried to study her Nursing 101 book, but every time she read a word associated with babies, she got horny. She also got curious. What did Buck like to do in the bedroom? How big was he below his belly button? Was his chest bare, like most white college girls said black men's chests were? Or, did he have those tightly curled, tiny knots of hair on his chest, like one cheerleader said? Her eyes wandered around the immaculate living room. Their fireplace sat empty, ready for a nice winter fire, although it was springtime. A Theodor Rombouts oil painting of the "Card Game," depicted four men in the background playing cards and one man playing a guitar in the foreground, hung over the luxury brown couch. So Buck's a gambling man. Finally, Brandy's curiosity won out. She went into the master bedroom to poke around.

She expected to see something different. Buck and Joycelynn's bedroom looked like any bedroom out of the JC Penny catalogue: king size bed, solid black, pink and yellow diamond pattern in orderly rows on the bedspread. Over the headboard, a painting of Monet's Water lilies. A tall mirror over a small chest, obviously for getting ready in the morning. Buck dressed neat and modest, like herself. Brandy turned around and looked at herself in the mirror. Today, she wore a University T-shirt over her bra and no-show, low-rise, black bikini. She blushed. She turned back and reached under the mattress, hoping to find Joycelynn's vibrator. She trailed her fingers around the entire bed length, until she reached what she thought was Buck's side. Hoping to find some porn magazines, but found nothing. "Probably in the chest drawers," Brandy thought hard. "Where would I put my sex stuff?"

She felt very naughty. The rush made

her nervous. Her belly tightened. Her pussy started to soak her bikini. "The bottom in the back." Brandy carefully pulled open the dark, cherry wood chest drawers, until it nearly dropped off. For a second, she studied the contents very carefully. She pointed and counted. Then she lifted one item of lingerie after another, until she found what she thought was a magazine. She slipped it out the side of the drawer. The plain white envelope was addressed to Buck.

Brandy hesitated. Then, she puckered the envelope that opened, not at the top, but the side. The white page fell out. "Two weeks ago," Brandy read the date. "Dear Buck. I am formerly filing for a divorce. I simply can't take your constant infidelity and sleeping around with other women. I know you have a thing for white bimbo girls. But sleeping with these young college women is going too far. I know you deny it. You will continue to deny it until the day you pass away. I simply don't care anymore, Buck. I know you're sleeping with Brandy, too. I see the way she leaves, all flushed skinned and excited. You can go on banging the babysitter for all I care. I am living with my mom now. I may come back for my things, when you and your white, college whore are not there. My lawyer will be calling you tomorrow! And he works really fast. Expect the papers next week!"

Brandy needed to plop down on the bed, but it was two feet away. She tottered over to it and started to sit down, then stopped. She moved over to a chair beside a tall bookcase, under a hanging black light fixture. She sat. Brandy believed in thinking things through. Buck hired me three weeks ago. I never had sex with him. He's never even approached me in any inappropriate manner. Not in words or innuendo. I've always dressed conservative. I never showed any skin. Not my feet or thighs, only my forearms and neck. I am not wearing a blouse attached to ruffles for my neck. This is the new millennium. I'm a modern girl. Maybe Buck slept with those other babysitters. I doubt it. From the one picture I saw, they all had deep tans. If Buck liked white girls, he'd go for a pale-is-beautiful girl first. Might as well go all the way white, if you're going to go white at all, Brandy figured. Like I go all the way black. Dark, midnight black, if I fucked anyone black at all.

Brandy flipped her left wrist over. "Fuck! Buck's going to be home in fifteen minutes! She hurried, as carefully as possible, to replace the letter. She staggered and sprang through the air on her feet into the full bathroom. Her hands pressed both sides of her face. She was flushed again. She slapped her face. "I'll tell Buck I was trying to keep myself awake studying." Her fingernails never concerned her. But, now that Buck was probably divorced already, she needed to paint them burgundy, or red, something to accentuate her pale white, glowing skin.

Six fifteen in the afternoon. Anger came over Brandy's round face. Her dimple in her chin made it seem like she was happy. Her blue, happy eyes registered a mildness. She pulled her short, ash-blonde hair behind her ears. "Since Joycelynn's already accused me of fucking Buck, I might as well fuck him, and have a good time at it. What a bitch! Accusing me of being a white-trash whore. What a bitch!"

At six-thirty, on the dot, the door lock turned and Buck announced himself. "Brandy, I'm home! Tawnequa, Daddy's here!"

Brandy came out and her smile relaxed Buck.

"Oh, how is our future Nanny doing today?"

"Hi Mr. Henderson, I'm doing fine. I had to slap myself on the face a couple times to stay awake, after Tawnequa took her nap..."

"Daddy! Daddy!" Tawnequa came

10

bouncing down the hallway from her room and leaped into six-foot Buck's arms.

Buck swung her around and kissed her on her cheeks several times. "How's my sweet and smart girl doing today? Did you read in school?"

"Mr. Henderson, I have to be going." Brandy apologized. "I have a Nanny 101 mid-term exam tomorrow."

"You will be here tomorrow, Brandy?" Mr. Henderson smiled. "We need your help, to keep our family running smoothly."

Brandy had one foot out the white door and one on the concrete level leading up to the house, "I will be here tomorrow."

"Say good-bye to the nice, smart nanny, Tawnequa." Mr. Henderson waved, as his five-year-old daughter waved.

Brandy clutched her college purse. She threw her blue backpack over her left shoulders. Her small lips made a smile on their own and her blue eyes blinked an extra long time. Brandy's hips seemed to undulate more than usual as she bustled down the walkway to her small, used burgundy Honda car.

Driving home, Brandy's emotions flew all over the place. Fear, because now her black fantasies most certainly might happen. Brandy realized if black men are as big as all her white girl friends said, she was going to have a terrible first time. She wasn't technically a virgin, but she's definitely never been fucked. "You'll know when you've been fucked," her girlfriends said. "And we can tell you've been dicked, but not fucked. You can't even get excited about your first sex experience."

Jimmy's penis didn't stretch her much, Brandy concluded. She remembered a little blood and all, on their first fucking, but she didn't cum. She didn't really cum. She didn't feel like screaming, "Fuck me! Fuck me, harder!" Like when she masturbated. The other white girls in her dorm said, "If you didn't beg for it again, you've never been fucked, Brandy!"

Brandy concluded, as she touched her pussy one last time, before going into her dorm room: I'm a virgin. If I do fuck Buck, and he's big and naughty, as mom says black men are, then I'm in for some sore, hard trouble.

Brandy slept, but her bed felt crowded. She kept hugging her pillow. One moment, she hugged it as if it was Buck. The next hour, she stuffed the king-sized pillow between her legs and shamelessly humped. Her thick calves twined around each other, adding more pressure between her wet thighs, as she pumped her cunt lips tight and hard around her slender clit, until her massive orgasms shook her body. She rode those orgasmic waves off into dreamland.

In her dorm room, warm feelings flowed through Brandy, as she set about to seduce Buck using her pretty, red painted toenails. Brandy wanted to jump in Buck's arms and yell, "Fuck this virgin white whore!" Of course, Mr. Buck Henderson's cool and refined demeaner stopped that. Buck's beyond such a crass attempt at seduction, Brandy surmised. How best to make him realize her sexual assets? Brandy thought her round 30B breasts might work, if she went braless. She might wear a cropped top and show her belly stud jewelry. Her round face might make him think of love. Sex needs to happen before love. "I know he's into white girls. What do I have...," Brandy wracked her brain.

"My feet." Buck had always stared at her gym shoes. "He has a foot fetish, I bet." And her pretty feet did have pedicures, because she often wore sandals like all the college girls in spring. Her pretty feet would lead him to her thick calves. White girls often have thicker calves than black girls do, Brandy secretly thought. This is what attracted black men. She'd find out tonight. Sandals said unprofessional, though. Mr. Henderson exuded class. So she pulled out a pair of her flowered, pink sling-back shoes. Her pretty toes showed. They slipped off easily. They can go almost anywhere. That's what

Brandy wore to pick up Tawnequa from school.

Brandy took off her flowered sling-back shoes and played with Tawnequa, and her girl Lego blocks, again. They built a castle, a spaceship, and a school. Brandy then read to Tawnequa about women scientists, when Tawnequa said, "Sometimes people who love each other separate."

"Give me a hug, Tawnequa." Brandy hugged the five-year-old. "Sometimes people find others who love them just as much, if not more."

"I'm sleepy, Brandy."

"Okay, how about a quick nap before Daddy comes home?" Tawnequa nodded her head.

Nervous, Brandy put Tawnequa to bed for her nap. Brandy Tuey studied her classwork to put out of her mind the possibility of fate intervening. Her clit drummed a steady beat inside her tight black jeans. She wore her light blue, silk boy-shorts and black v-neck blouse. She thought her boy-shorts might take the sexiness off her thoughts. They didn't.

When Buck came home, he called out to Brandy and Tawnequa. Usually Tawnequa runs out, down the hallway, and jumps into her Daddy's arms. Today she remained asleep.

"I guess Tawnequa's tired out from her busy day. We read about women scientists." Brandy pointed, "And she built a castle, a school, and a spaceship."

Buck laughed. "How much building did you do, Brandy?" He looked at her and smiled. His broad smile made Brandy feel confident.

"Fifty percent only." Brandy laughed. Brandy's eyes darted down at her feet. She stood there in her sling-backs and Buck noticed right away.

"I think I've struck gold with you, Brandy." Buck stole a glance down at her pretty pedicures.

Brandy started to pack up her blue backpack. "Well, I think I'd better be going, Mr. Henderson."

Buck brought his eyes slowly over Brandy's entire body. "Have a seat, Brandy."

Brandy sat on the couch with her bookbag. Buck sat on the side chair. He leaned back in the chair and stretched his legs. "Did Tawnequa ask about her mom?"

"Uhm. Yes. I mean... no, Mr. Henderson." Brandy crossed her legs toward Buck. She let her sling-back sandal dangle from her left foot.

"You should know Joycelynn and I have been divorced now, for three weeks," Buck started. "We still need a babysitter." He smiled when Brandy's small blue eyes beamed. The dimple came back into her chin. "Some days, Tawnequa will stay with

Joycelynn."

Brandy sat back and considered this. A rush of excitement and defeat flowed into her veins. All over her body, she throbbed with electricity. Buck likes white girl's feet. "I was right," Brandy thought.

"That reminds me," Buck reached into his pocket.

Brandy noticed how huge his cock was, now that his pants stretched tight across his waist. If she fucked Buck, he'd rip her to shreds. She practically flooded her quivering cunt.

"Here's your weekly pay."

Brandy went to reach his hand, when her sandal fell off. She put her barefoot forward, leaned, and got the cash. "Next week?" She sat back and slowly, sensuously, slipped on her shoe.

He put both hands behind his head. "Three days a week."

"That still helps a lot, Mr. Henderson." She paused, her eyebrows moved together. "I'd like to ask you something."

"Sure, go ahead, Brandy."

"Want to fuck me?"

Buck Henderson's eyes widened. He still held his clasps hand behind his head. "You mean, like my wife has been accusing me of?"

"She has?"

"You read the divorce letter?"

Brandy laughed, "I'm a poor spy."

"Lipstick."

Brandy had only recently begun to wear lipstick. She liked her natural, fresh face look. "Oh."

"I never slept with any of those other babysitters," he lowered his hands to his lap. "I know I have a thing for white girls, and white girls have a sex thing for me."

"Oh, you're not alone wanting to fuck the opposite race, Mr. Henderson... Buck." Brandy kicked off her flowery sling-back shoes and raised one foot on the luxury brown couch. Her crotch pointed right at Buck. She knew he could see the small wet spot soaking through her jeans. "I've wanted to fuck a black boy, or man, since I was fourteen."

Buck laughed. "It's a common fantasy, doing the opposite race."

"It's my addiction," she smiled hesitantly and unbuttoned her black v-neck blouse. "I'm still practically a virgin."

Buck unbuckled his belt, as Brandy listened to one of her fantasies coming true. The sound of a man undressing drove her wild with lust. "I don't want to be some white-trash whore, though, Buck. We have to be an item."

Buck's white shorts barely contained his growing black dick meat. "I want a relationship. If you noticed, Tawnequa's room has an extra bed." He rubbed his black dong through his underwear. "I want another girl for Tawnequa to play with. A sister."

Brandy considered this. She reached inside her blouse and flicked her nipples back and forth, making them hard. She saw the pink little pebbles harden and visibly show through her black v-neck blouse. Buck licked his lips and groaned. Brandy unbuttoned her jeans. She wore no belt, like most girls. Her jeans were so tight they stayed on her frame, like a second skin. Her black boy-shorts showed. She lifted her hips and shimmied her jeans to her ankles.

Brandy waited, anxiously, for Buck to make the first move. Her fear of his size frightened her. She didn't want to tell him she needed his reassurance of her beauty, worth, and her fuckability. She might disappoint him being she fucked only once.

Buck stood up, lowered his black dress pants, took off his expensive dress shoes, came over to Brandy, and carefully lifted her jeans off her pretty peds.

Brandy loved the confident look in his medium brown eyes. His nose flared, only a little at the base. His calmness made her cream. His dark mustache was clean and neat. She could not wait to feel his mustache tickling her clitoris and inner pussy lips. She couldn't wait to grab his short cut, tightly curled hair in her hands and force his tongue deeper into her swollen pussy. She'd finally get to see what kind of chest hair he had.

Once he had her jeans down and off her ankles, he began loving her. Buck's wide lips gingerly kissed her feet. His tongue darted out, only slowly, like a shy snake sniffing its surroundings. Hot and electric! He licked on her clean, pretty feet and pedicure toes. Brandy threw her slender legs wide over the couch armrest and pushed her sex into his face. Her soaked, black boy-shorts making a sexy, slick camel-toe. Buck began to eat her pussy.

He ate her pussy first, through her shorts. Then he ate her pussy naked. Afterwards, he pulled down his white shorts and his thick, eight and half-inch midnight cock came into view. He was as wide around as Brandy's wrist.

Brandy pulled back thinking, and commented unsteadily, "Oh, this is a mistake. I can't take it. It's too big, Buck."

"Brandy," Buck said in his reassuring Management Consultant voice. "You have to take some risk to get at all the pleasure."

Brandy nodded. Buck helped her pull up her black v-neck.

"You're a dream girl, Brandy." He looked over her spherical breasts, nice B sized, and his massive black hands held them perfectly. He mauled her nipples under his fingers. He lowered his mouth to her right tit. "Brandy...?"

"I agree, Buck!" she heaved and sighed. "Let's take this into the bedroom."

In the bedroom, Buck took Brandy's virginity a second time. More blood spilt from her sore split, because she never had anyone his size. When it was all over the first time, Brandy wanted to fuck, again. "Fuck me. Fuck me harder and faster this time, Buck!" She taunted him, "I want to feel it. Fuck me!"

They fucked three times that night, and Brandy felt too sore to attend her classes. She was determined to keep going to school. She, Buck, and Tawnequa made a nice new family. Brandy got so used to being at Mr. Henderson's place, her girlfriends knew she had been fucked and found a man! "Now you're one of the big girls," said the cheerleader in her dorm suite. "Fucking a black man's got to be the top fantasy to act out."

Her girlfriends almost had it right. Brandy was in love, too. Buck loved her back. Tawnequa was pleased to have a nanny at home every day. It all came so easily for Brandy. Fate intervened, she concluded.

"Buck! Buck!" Brandy ran into the study where he was reading "The

Management of Society and Social Networking." She went around and sat on his lap. Her happy blue eyes smiled as wide as her tiny eyes could. Her dimpled chin quivered.

"What is it Brandy, tell me?" His massive hands held her gently. "You're..."

"I am!"

"We're going to have a child!"

"A girl, just like you wanted, Buck!"

"I can't believe it."

"My gyno says it's very unusual for a girl to get preggo on her first fuck."

"You are one lucky virgin white girl." He paused, "Does your gyno know your lover is black?"

Brandy raised her black polka dot dress up over her slender white thighs.

"No panties."

"Only for you, not the gyno." Brandy reached back and unlocked Buck Henderson's monster tool. "Yes, he does, Buck. I told him. He did not frown or anything. Stretch me some more, Buck. Make me sore."

Buck pulled out his cock and it grew faster, thicker, harder, and looked mean.

Brandy marveled at the thick veins on the underside. His cock head was like a helmet; round and ready to pierce her small cunt. He held her weightlessly in his strong black arms. Brandy struggled to make his precum-spewing, massive dick

ERIC RESHER

fit inside her. She put pressure on his dickhead forcing it between her lips. Buck did the rest and gently pulled her down on his loving hard member.

She buried her face in Buck's corded neck, leaning back on his bare chest. "Buck, I've made wedding plans."

"That's fine. Just give me two weeks advance notice."

"It's tomorrow!"

"On a Friday? That's my card game night. You're kidding."

"I want to keep your black cock forever," Brandy said huffing. She lifted up and stuffed that thick, black cock of Buck's down her pussy alley, again.

He pushed up inside her to the max and stopped. "Brandy, this is serious. I don't take marriage lightly."

That was all Brandy needed to hear. She fucked Buck with complete abandon. "Seriously, Buck."

"I guess I'll have to postpone the card came until next month."

Brandy Tuey and Buck Henderson got married the next day by a judge in the court.

2 PLAYING CARDS FOR BRANDY

Brandy Tuey sat naked on a fluffy and soft pink towel in their bedroom at her own writing desk. Loud techno music played in the background, as she thought warmly how Buck insisted she continue to study for her Nanny/Nursing Degree, to finish the year out. "No wife of mine is going to strut around illiterate. Even though my dad was a plumber, he made sure I graduated from college. And you will too, Brandy." A slice of pepperoni pizza, half eaten on a white napkin, flavored the room. Spring flowers bloomed outside, and birds chirped in the warmer breezes. Brandy continued to bloom into her second month of pregnancy. Her sexy baby bump would be a month away. That didn't stop Brandy from munching her pizza and composing a letter to her mom.

Friday, May 13, 2011
Dear Mom,
All those terrible sexual things you warned me about materialized. I went to the University, studied for nearly a year, got a job as a babysitter, and got knocked up. Now, I'm pregnant by this black guy. It's terrible Mom. We fucked because, like you said, Mom, I needed a black cock and was worth only the sex between my slender legs and thick calves. On the first night, I cried, "Ooooh, it's big." On the second night of passion, I cried, "That's a long fellow." The third night of passion I cried, "What a hot long tongue licking me!" For night four, we repeated night three and I cried, "Yesss, eat my creaming white pussy, black guy!" Our fifth night, we did all the things completed the previous four nights, Mom. I even got down on my knees, before his powerful black thighs and groin. And I mean black, Mom. He couldn't be any more blacker than I am white. I got down on my knees. I pulled the B cups of my black T-shirt bra aside, letting Buck soak in my beautiful round spherical breasts. I wore no panties, Mom. Guess what? I used no hands, too. I sucked on that delicious piece of sexy black cock, all the way down

my throat. I held on to his thighs. Honestly, Mom, I thought of gagging, but was determined not to. You know I'm a stubborn girl. What you didn't accept was that I am loving, caring, and like to be needed by others. I like to make others happy. So, heck no, I did not gag. I deep throated my black-skinned lover. I rolled my tongue around that monster penis. I am now, according to your standards, all used up and a useless white piece of whore trash. I am glowing in that sexual glow twenty-four hours a day. I'm sitting here at my own office desk, in our plush bedroom, naked. My fuck hole is so sore, and pouring out all his black semen on a thick pink towel. He is at work as a Management Consultant. He guides others in running their businesses. He has class. He wants me to have class and finish my degree.

Besides all those dire things you wished on me, do not worry I cannot get pregnant, Mom. I am most certainly protected, because I am already certified knocked up and preggo. No matter how careful I was, Mom, my gyno said I was one fertile woman anyway. Just the hint of a black man's sperm might impregnate me, he said. It was fate, and bound to happen, Mom. I didn't go out to meet big, black Buck. Fate presented him on a silver platter at my feet.

We watch black on white porno films, too. You should be proud now, Mom. You raised a proper white girl who loves to fuck black cocks!

Your loving, alabaster daughter, who loves fucking black men,

Signed, Brandy the Babysitter

P.S. I am his Princess (those are Buck Henderson's words) and Buck is my Prince. We married last month, by a Judge in the court. I reside in a huge house with a modest sized living room and kitchen, large bedroom with a small bathroom inside it, children's room, full bathroom, and a powder room. There's even a near regulation size swimming pool in the back. We read the classics in the den, go to museums, plays, symphonies and all that boring shit I never got to do when I grew up in that trailer park.

Brandy's 30B spherical breasts jiggled back and forth, as she wrote. Her nipples hardened. Her thick calves steadied her feet from wanting to run and jump back into bed and fuck herself silly. Her dripping pussy couldn't wait for Buck to get home. After pressing the self-sealing envelope shut, Brandy jumped into the hot shower and let the silky water run all over the length of her average height body. Water poured over her short, blonde hair and small eyes. Her arched eyebrows gave Brandy a rather sophisticated look, when she didn't smile. Her small lips made her chin dimple unforgettable. Her round face directed attention to the feminine hollow of her neck.

Brandy let the water flow over her neck, through the hollow and down, over her 30B breasts. Her nipples turned a dark pink under the hot water. Brandy's resistance broke down, as the silky water flowed like thousands of loving hands over her entire body. She was only five feet, six-inches. As she moved, her belly jewelry sparkled. Below that, from her perpendicular perspective, her clit bump showed itself. Brandy mused, after five months, she'll no longer be able to see her clit bump. After seven months, her feet will be mysterious things that allowed her to glide through the world. At nine months, she'll be a wobbling, happy Momma whale.

Brandy went on a pink shopping spree and bought some sexy negligees, crotchless panties, and peek-a-boo bras. Towards the end of her shopping, Brandy focused more on sexy preggo clothing, like a pink nighty with six white bows as buttons and some crotchless panties, and a nursing bra in particular. Her tits started growing fuller and bigger. The pressure on her skin made her as horny as a young girl growing her first boobies. As she walked around the famous lingerie shop, Brandy's mind raced with desire, as she sampled several slinky items. Another woman shopped for herself, too, named Heidi. Heidi told Brandy, "I run maternity parties for women. If you ever want to attend one, just call."

Brandy turned over the pink and blue card and finally stuck it in her purse. She returned her thoughts to Buck. How kind and generous Buck was last month, postponing his monthly Friday night card game with his five black buddies from college. Before meeting and marrying Buck, she didn't know why she never watched any black on white interracial porno films. She watched the Maxtrix, and thousands of interracial couples populated that movie trilogy. Interracial sex was a force coming and no one could stop it. Sure, the entire world would never integrate. That might destroy the fun of interracial sex, if everyone blended! But now, that's all she wanted to watch. So many ideas flowed through her mind. Brandy knew Buck thought the same thing as she. They loved seeing one white woman servicing five black cocks. Brandy didn't want to bring it up, when she realized how close to fulfilling this babysitter fantasy of hers might be.

She dreamed up a fantasy long ago of babysitting for a rich white couple at their spacious mansion. Just as she prepared to leave the already starting party, one light-skinned black man propositioned her. So, she went into one of the many bedrooms in this huge house. Then, as she fucked him, another darker, medium brown, black man came into the room. She didn't want to leave, because this man was darker than the last. She fucked them both. The door opened again and one darker brown black man entered. Of course, Brandy had to have him as well. On her fantasy went. In her dream, she must have fucked twenty black men that night. Until she fucked the last blue-black man, who swung the biggest, thickest, burgeoning erection she could imagine. This made Brandy desire a black man more than ever. Luckily, she met Buck. Big, wide, hung long, blue-blue-blackest man she ever laid eyes on. Brandy dared not tell all this fantasy to her husband. She suspected he had similar fantasies, but didn't know how to present them to her, too.

"Brandy," Buck said, hours before the card game began. "Want to make our own black on white fuck tape?"

Brandy sashayed up to Buck and leaned into his massive arms. "What wicked thing do you have in that smart brain of yours?"

"All you have to do is act like you're asleep."

"Asleep?"

"Each of my buddies won't resist wanting to fuck you."

"If I was nude..."

"Nude!"

"We want to prevent any missed opportunities, right, Buck?" Buck thought it over. "Bright idea. I'll position the hidden camera. I won't say where it is. I want you to act natural." Buck hugged Brandy and he felt her trembling against his body.

Brandy knew Buck loved and trusted her to allow this. Even though she felt his heart racing like mad, she felt a sense of calm confidence in him. Now, she was going to lay naked as Venus in their master bedroom, as five black, strange men (to her anyway) came in and fucked her. How do men pull off this strange, exciting stuff? Brandy wondered. Did he just say, "Ahem, you guys can fuck my wife, but don't get out of hand?" The anticipation did a dance number on her pussy lips, clit, and beady nipples. Her ivory skin begged to be touch by those strange black hands. She couldn't wait until their big, black balls bounced off her sweaty ass cheeks. She and Buck would watch this fuck flick more than any, in their growing stash of porn tapes.

Brandy had taken a nice clean bath, wore her favorite perfume, Eternity by CK, and waited, curled up on their king sized bed... Naked!

Hours later, Buck's college friends began to come in. Brandy heard the high fives and trash talk about postponing the card game last month. They talked about women they were dating and bragged on their sexual exploits. Brandy's pussy kept opening and closing. She felt like a virgin all over again. Suddenly, she thought about having Buck using velcro handcuffs and locking her spread arms and legs to the bed's post. Then, the men would know she's available. She stored that idea for another time. The men sat in the living room. She heard Buck pull the large table from the nearby den into the living room area, arranging chairs with two of the guy's help. They turned on the large flat screen television, embedded in the wall, across from the luxury brown couch. Brandy heard the beer cans open. A basketball game played loud on the cable channel. Brandy wasn't much of a television watcher, herself. She realized television zapped one's brain of its mental power. She refused to let Tawnequa get addicted to television. Outside of Sesame Street, Mister Roger's, and a few Discovery Channel programs on science, Brandy banned all television from the six year old.

Television was now her best friend... For porno tapes, anyway. Brandy got a little concerned, because Buck didn't show her where the hidden camera was. She did not know where to look into it and show Buck she's willingly thrilled, as his black buddy's cocks drilled her white pussy into having a good time

More than that, Brandy tried to figure out how to act asleep during orgasms. How to not direct a guy to push in harder, or faster, when he fucked her too slow? What a strange task. The things she did for black fuck meat. This waiting stimulated her more than all the fucking in her rich dream imagination. Eventually, Brandy listened hard and kept stroking her engorged pussy lips. She was pinching her clit like there would be no tomorrow. Brandy sorted out Buck's friends one by one:

Suhuba, the friendly one, never got a lot of white pussy. He worked at a black social service agency, helping the poor and needy find homes. He was the tallest. Brandy thought his cock might match his height. She didn't possess the extensive experience of her college girlfriend and dorm hall mate, the cheerleader, though. Maybe height didn't match cock size. Finger size matched cock size and Buck had thick long fingers. Suhuba wanted to get married someday.

Akbar's voice boomed and he talked volumes about the white pussy he's scored. Rich white pussy and poor white trash, like herself. Even middle class, home girl, white-picket fence, Mom-you'd like to fuck white girls. Brandy squeezed her spherical tits and twisted her nipples waiting for his deep dark voice to enter the bedroom. She had to practice different ways to act as if she were asleep. Each man might approach her differently. She suspected Akbar might be the most direct. He certainly talked as if he was the most confident of Buck's friends. Akbar used to play for a semi-professional football league, until he found a sports medicine job paying twice the salary, with no risk of permanent, physical injury. He was married and divorced. "I can't stay with one woman, Buck. I don't have the skills to settle down." Brandy found herself thinking if she even wanted Akbar inside her precious pussy after that comment. Then she realized, he was every white girl's fantasy. Someone to fuck and forget about bringing home to Mommy or Daddy.

Rex had dark brown skin, said Suhuba. Rex claimed to be a charmer. He never fucked a girl; he made love to her. Brandy adored Rex, but her white girlfriends pfffff on guys who claimed to be lovers. Those are the worse kind, they warned innocent Brandy. Rex ran his own warehousing business for machine parts. He and Buck had done business before, across the negotiating table.

Finally, Hagen, the youngest and lightest one they called "Biscuit." "Hmmm," Brandy thought. He wasn't black, but bi-racial, like Buck's and her girl child would be, bi-racial when born seven months from now. He taught school in a public school in a poor white trash neighborhood. He claimed the M.I.L.Fs tossed their panties at his feet whenever he sat at parent-teacher's conferences. Brandy laughed. No mom, even white-trash moms, would do that. Or do they? Brandy suspected her Mom fucked a black guy long ago.

After thirty-minutes of waiting, Brandy's drooling, horny pussy left a huge wet spot under her ass, still in the fetal position. She began to think this would never happen. "I'm waiting and waiting." That's when Suhuba announced, "Deal me out of this hand. Time to use the little boy's room."

"Buck, don't deal me out of this hand. Time for me to use the...men's room," Akbar said in that powerful, deep voice that made Brandy's pussy liquefy more of her pent up desires.

The two men briefly argued, before Buck said, "Flip a coin. Winner uses the men's room first."

"Cool, Buck," Suhuba said quietly.

Akbar retorted. "I'm the man," he pointed to himself down below his belt, "And to show you, I'm going to allow you to go first. Only if you win!" His deep voice emphasized, "Only if you win." Akbar laughed scornfully at Suhuba.

Brandy's tits tightened every time she heard Akbar's massive voice.

"Drum roll Rex and Hagen," Buck ordered.

The two men rapidly and loudly began drumming on the table top with such expert precision that Brandy wondered what squeezing, pulling, twisting and pinching Rex and Hagen's nimble fingers might do all over her body, also.

"Call it," Buck shouted, as the coin turned over and over in the air.

Brandy felt as if they were flipping to see who gets to fuck her fresh pussy first. She felt like a helpless white girl, in a harem of all black men. Once, in a history class, she'd seen a film of this. Her first small orgasm hit her slender body. An average white-trash woman going on an epic sexual adventure, soon to begin, rolled on her brain cells, firing back and forth the length of her body, sending electric currents to strange places Brandy never considered sexual. She caressed her neck. She wanted to see if her skin sex flush started. Brandy drew her knees up

35

to her breasts tighter.

"Tails."

"Heads," came the loud, sonic boom from Akbar.

Buck's calm, right hand caught the coin and slapped it over, onto the back of his left hand.

"Heads."

"Ha... Hey! Ha... Hey! Didn't I say I was the man!" Akbar boomed, turned, and went into the living room bathroom.

Defeated, Suhuba said, "Buck, I can't wait, man."

"Then, why don't you use the bathroom in my bedroom."

Rex smirked, "Suhuba stop jumping up and down like a little child."

"You serious, Buck?" Suhuba said.

Buck nods his head, looked Suhuba in the eye, calm and assured. He continued shuffling the cards, "Go ahead, Brandy is two months pregnant and sleeps like a boulder. She even took a sedative. So she is fast asleep. If it sounds like she's awake, I assure you she's still asleep. We even fuck like that sometimes. She wants me to take her when she's asleep."

Suhuba rushed into the bedroom. He zipped in so fast, he banged the door and it rebounded, and shut. He looked straight ahead. There laid Brandy, like a virgin goddess, curled up in the fetal position. Her naked ass and sandwiched meaty pussy lips facing the door. He turned around as the door clicked. He grabbed his crotch and all the piss felt like it ran backwards, up his urethra. His cock forgot about pissing and wanted to do some fucking. "Shit man. Whoah!" He ran into the bathroom and started to piss on the toilet seat. But, remembering the beautiful sight moments before, he lifted the white toilet seat and disgorged his semi-erect, five-inches of cock of its dark yellow piss. He flushed the toilet. He stared at himself in the mirror. "What the fuck is going on? Buck must want me to fuck his wife." Suhuba flushed the toilet, dried his hands on the blue towel, and came back out. He stepped twice toward the door, but couldn't resist Brandy's siren call. She moaned.

Brandy reached back toward the door. Then, slapped the hand back on her stark white hip. Her hips rolled and squirmed.

Suhuba decided to go closer. He could smell pussy. He smelled her heat. His desire practically ran out and dragged him over to her naked white body. "Man, oh man."

Suhuba reached out and stopped. He reached out again. He slowly and softly touched her slender thighs. He marveled at the beauty of her thick white calves. "She's got to be part German, with them beautiful thick calves," Suhuba whispered.

Brandy suppressed a quiver and her pussy gushed at the first touch on her thighs. She had German heritage. Czech heritage, too.

He pulled back his hand, reached forward, and dipped his finger into her wet gash. He finally noticed the pool of her pussy oil below. "She's hot. Fucking marvelous." Suhuba licked his fingers and smelled her sweet, tangy scent.

Suhuba, the darkest of them all, with his African sounding name, deserved first dibs. Brandy wouldn't have wanted it any other way. He unbuckled his pants and pushed them to his ankles. He knelt carefully on the bed. Leaning in, he pushed his cock, all seven and a half-inches, into Brandy's waiting cunt. Brandy moaned. Suhuba couldn't believe she didn't wake. He pushed slow and easy, in and out. He grabbed her hips and thighs, and brought Brandy toward his crotch. He wished he had her on her knees and hands, doggy style. That's when Brandy turned over on her stomach and put her hands under her face.

Suhuba literally fell into her pussy. He sank into her soft, succulent flesh and nearly shuttered there. He lay on top of Buck's beautiful white wife and she lay there motionless. He developed a quick rhythm. Then, hearing Akbar come out of the other bathroom, Suhuba pumped harder and came in a rush of relief. He wanted to kiss Brandy's white shoulder. He loved that she had no tattoos to mar her gorgeous, luminous white skin. He pulled out and saw her hips twist and her pussy seemed to push his white come right out. It pooled under, between her legs. Suhuba quickly dressed and left.

Hagen and Rex gave Suhuba a curious look of envy. Akbar came out, oblivious to everything.

"How was the little 'boys' room, Su-hu-ba!" Akbar bragged.

"Nice. I feel like a real man, now."

"Just like a wimp," his deep voice continued.

Rex said, "All these beers are getting me, too. I have to go use the restroom as well."

"Sorry Rex," Akbar announced. "I killed the fucking living room bathroom. It's flooded. Number 2." He laughed. "Call the Rotor Hooter, or whatever over, those pipes are weak. You couldn't flush a cotton ball down that, Buck."

Buck had rigged the living room bathroom. His father worked the plumber's trade and showed him about the water pressure, behind the toilet.

"Use the extra one in my bedroom, Rex." Buck hesitated and gave him a knowing look. They had done business before. Rex ran a warehousing business and Buck engaged in a negotiation, or two, with him.

"Sure thing, Buck." Rex entered the door and closed it right afterwards. He noticed Brandy lying on her belly, turned slightly to the side. White cum flowed out of her wet gash, her gasping briefly, with a satisfied pussy. She looked wonderful and, as if it was a dream, Rex floated over to her slender, average body, built like the Goddess Venus. His eyes focused on her thick, German calves. "No black women have thick calves like that," he whispered. Rex stopped and looked for a hidden camera. Not finding any, he let his hand drift up from her calves, all the way to her hips.

Brandy suddenly turned over and her 30B-27-35 form laid naked for him to admire. "Oh gosh." Brandy had thrown one elbow over her eyes. From under them, she saw Rex's growing cock.

Rex unbuckled his pants and stood naked from the waist down. "Buck said he fucked her when she's slept." Rex crawled onto the bed and lifted up Brandy's flushed thighs. "She's not going to be fat after her pregnancy. What a body." Rex put himself between her thighs and slowly inched his cock into her wet pussy. He held her spread legs on his hips. He looked down and watched all the clear pussy fluids. He surmised this was Brandy's desire and the white cream, which he concluded was Suhuba's cum, oozed out. Rex closed his eyes in pleasure.

Brandy peaked out from under her elbows as she stifled a moan from her lips by biting on her tongue. Brown-skinned Rex wasn't as dark as Suhuba, but Rex's girth matched a little over Buck's. Brandy strained and was glad Rex wasn't first, or she might have given up the game and cried out in painful ecstasy. She could barely get her hand around Buck's fuck rod. Here is Rex, practically fisting her. His black, battering ram cock was wider in circumference than her wrist. Was such a cock legal? Gosh, it went on forever, Rex getting inside her pussy. Then, it took forever for her pussy to let go of Rex's mammoth staff. Finally, her pussy understood how to accommodate him. They got into a nice rhythm. Brandy realized playing being asleep allowed her to feel every muscle in her body in a new way. She luxuriated in feeling her round, young breasts rise and fall as Rex pushed into her and pulled out. Occasionally, Rex reached up and caressed his right hand across both her tits. His nimble hands mauled her right breast, tweaked her nipple, and darted to her left breast, repeating the touch of fire on her flesh. Her nipples increased their tension on the down jerk and relaxed on the up push. She never concentrated on her nipples while running, but she imagined this must be what they feel like. Her hips stretched wider, as Rex leaned into her V and her clit popped out at every little ending entry bang. Rock and roll took on a sexual meaning like never before. It felt great. She felt nasty and dirty, allowing all these black men to use her body. Rex playfully felt up her ass, gripping and groping her buoyant, soft, alluring white flesh.

Brandy laughed to herself. She didn't have to do anything to make it seem like she was fucking. All her fucking motions were covered by her jiggling tits and flat belly rolling, like waves coming and leaving a beach, as Rex push-banged into her. Her interior pussy muscles did a dance number around Rex's wide girth, once she figured out how to relax and fuck him. He was none the wiser. He kept whispering, "What a tight, young pussy. What a young, tight pussy." Brandy rocked faster and concentrated on keeping her elbow over her face as Rex finally released his black, lewd desires up her love hole and fell off the side of her. He quickly dressed and flushed the toilet, after wiping the wide girth of his dick with some toilet paper.

He opened the door, and nodded to Buck.

"All well in there, Rex?" Buck asked, calmly.

"All good, buddy. Thanks."

Akbar seemed puzzled. "What the fuck is going on?" He studied all five faces. "I have to use the bathroom again. Damn beer manufacturers."

"Behave yourself, Akbar," Buck warned.

Akabar said, "Oh man, you need to call your Dad over to fix that lame commode." Akabar went into the bedroom, looked to the right of the bathroom, and went straight to the toilet. He pissed. He came out and saw Brandy, naked. He stopped in his tracks.

He dropped his pants by the bathroom door and crept over to Brandy. Flushed skinned Brandy looked like she was smiling and sleeping. Her face turned to the side, facing the window, away from the door. Her legs lay across the bed, feet facing the door. Akbar, seeing all the cum, knew he had been cockled. He was getting sloppy thirds.

When Brandy saw him, from under her semi-closed eyelids, she smiled and knew the game probably was up. She couldn't help tossing her hands up and caressing both her 30B breasts, in a reflective desire. Then, she dropped both hands by her sides. Akbar said, "I'm going to hit this white pussy, too."

Akbar had nine inches of live dick and

this huge cap across the top. Brandy couldn't wait to get him inside her. But how? She wanted him to turn her over, doggy style. She kept saying it over and over. "Doggy style, Akbar... Doggy style."

Akbar started to do one thing and stopped. Then, he didn't know what to do. "Fucking Cover Girl, nice round face. Look at that sexy dimple in her chin." He grabbed Brandy's legs and said, "Fuck this!" He twisted her legs, causing Brandy to make a "Gumph" sound. Then, he pulled Brandy back onto his hip. She lay limp, waiting.

"What the fuck," Brandy thought. She lay on her stomach. He had her in his hands. Her legs were now around his black waist. "Stick that black, nine-inch pussy splitter up my muff," Brandy thought.

Akbar realized he had a logistical problem. He squatted lower. Placing his boner at the mouth of her sex, in just an inch, Brandy rolled her hips upward and he slipped out. Akabar tried again. He squatted, placed his sex at her lips, and pulled her back on him, about three inches. Then he lifted her hips up higher and pushed her body forward, so that Brandy now rested on her left shoulder. Brandy made a moaning sound and placed her elbows crossed under her face, while Akbar achieved his desire.

Akbar went as deep as he could into Brandy's young white cunt.

Brandy sighed and sighed, as Akbar kept pushing his inches into her, five-inches.

Brandy sighed,

Six-inches.

Brandy sighed.

Seven-inches,

Brandy sighed,

Eight-inches.

Brandy tried to sigh, but grunted.

Nine-inches, Brandy said, "Oohhh, That's good, fuck me, fuck me, fuck . . ." and let her voice trail off.

Akbar figured she didn't sleep like a stone. He pounded Brandy's pussy for a good three minutes, before releasing his progenitors into her white pussy gash to go ova hunting. He pulled out and watched her clutching, white, wet snatch, puckering so hard. Brandy's ass hole moved visibly in and out, in and out.

He ran, picked up his pants, and left.

"Your turn, Hagen," Buck offered.

Hagen, the youngest, had no clue. As he entered the room, he knew right away. Brandy offered herself to them, with Buck's knowledge apparently. Now, he'd finally get some white pussy after all.

Brandy knelt there, in a deep doggy style pose, on the bed. Her legs spread wide apart in a V and her love juices, with the cum of three other black men drooled down from her love palace, onto the bed.

Hagen lost no time. He took off his pants and positioned himself behind Brandy. He pulled her white, curved hips toward him. He pushed her legs together. "We're going to make this pussy tight as can be." He spread his legs outside of Brandy's legs. Her stark, white thighs inside his light skin black thighs. Her thick white calves inside his black calves.

Brandy had no idea what he was talking about. Her pussy gapped so much, she couldn't keep the air out of it. She felt open and free. When Hagen pushed her legs together, her pelvic muscles tightened. Her pussy shut. Hagen pushed in with his seven-inch cock. Brandy cried in ecstasy, as Hagen fought his way inside her sloppy wet pussy valley. She was tighter. She loved it. She hoped to see this on camera.

Brandy pulled the far away king-sized pillow under her face and rocked with Hagen. She bit into that pillow to stifle her screams of pleasure. She came with a huge crash of multiple orgasms. She wanted to throw her legs apart, heave, huff, and pop and roll.

His hands went everywhere, all over Brandy's body, like a salmon. Hagen stroked her belly. He brushed against her drumming clit. He patted her juicy ass cheeks. He rubbed her sides. "Bet you wanna spread them pretty German calves and thighs." Hagen said in a balmy soft voice.

Brandy desperately desired just that. She kept biting into the pillow. Her 30B breasts rubbed the sheet, and rubbed her tiny pink nipples, until she came again and again. She felt sweaty and lusty all over.

Hagen came. He leaned over her white ass and gentle-slight hourglass hips. He wanted to kiss her back, and did. Brandy rewarded him by squeezing his cock one last time. Hagen's cock understood and spurted one last time. Then, slipped out. Hagen stumbled and leaned on Brandy, pushing her off to her side. She laid there, in the fetal position, again with a smile on her face. She had achieved one of her babysitting fantasies, but she had a lot more where that came from in her dirty mind.

Brandy fell asleep after Hagen.

"You're right, Buck. Your wife is sleeping like a mountain. I pulled out my dick and waved it around standing by the doorway and she didn't even wake up."

All the guys, and Buck, laughed. The card game ended in a couple of hours and the four college buddies drove home.

Brandy listened as the four cars left. "Buck! Buck!"

Buck came in and saw his wife, Brandy, laying back. Her skin flushed pink, all over, and her pussy still gaping wide, swollen, as she had her legs spread wide, her feet on the bed. She lay in a bowel size pool of male sperm and female pussy pleasure juices. "Those buddies of yours are naughty. They took advantage of your wife," she pouted. "What are you going to do about it, Buck?"

Buck unsnapped his pants and said, "I'm going to fuck those four guys right out of your memory. The only black cock you're going to remember, Brandy, is mine. Get in the doggy style position. So I can fuck dat pussy dry."

Brandy eagerly knelt into the doggy style position. Four black men's cum came gushing out of her highway pussy and Buck didn't complain. "I've got it all on camera wench. I'm the best at banging the babysitter and don't you forget that, Brandy. My wife."

"My pleasure, Buck."

3 BRANDY'S BUBBLE BATH ADVENTURE

Beautiful, ivory skinned Brandy sat on the burlap wrapped square stools at their kitchen table. Again, she didn't have any clothes on. "I like being nude," she mused to herself. "I should find a nudist colony or club somewhere." Brandy began to write another letter to her mom.

Friday, June 11, 2011

Dear Mom,

I love you. I just love black cock in my white pussy more! I'm three months preggo now. My sex glow is amazing. My belly bump is showing. Mom, I'm sitting here in our full kitchen on burlap wrapped stools, at our granite tabletop. It's so pretty, Mom. All the black dots on the white surface reminds me of black coffee and white cream. The window looks out over our pool. I am nude, again, Mom. I've discovered that I like being nude. Is that another thing on your list of disgusting activities and habits? Being nude? We were all born nude, Mom. I am sitting on a thick, soft, white towel, which I must say is doing a playful number on my bald cunt.

Buck is working on a major Management Consultant Project. What is a Management Consultant, you ask, Mom? Management Consultants advise people on how to best use their company's resources; workers, systems, products and procedures. He also trains personnel in new procedures. See Mom, it all started with a guy name Mr. Wedgwood. Josiah Wedgwood, to be exact. He ran a pottery business back in the 1700s. Ha! Mom, that's way before your time. So, all that talk you told me about how my worthless playing with clay wouldn't amount to anything was another lie. Mr. Wedgwood became famous making clay pots. Mr. Wedgwood birthed the concept of mass-producing items of uniform quality. Sort of like Mr. Ford's assembly line of cars, in Detroit. I'm sure you can understand that, Mom.

Buck does the same thing. He helps people. Buck makes $60,000 a year, easily, Mom. He is working harder to make more money, since we have child, Pomona, *on the way. Pomona means Goddess of fruit trees and products. Pomona and Tawnequa are going to be best friends forever.*

So, I hope you're satisfied. Your white daughter's creamy twat enjoys dark chocolate candy cock.

Your loving alabaster daughter who loves fucking black men,

Signed, Brandy the Babysitter

Brandy reasoned that since her mom hated black men, she must constantly tell her that Buck's a good man, and is providing for her. Obviously, her Mom wants to believe the worst of our relationship. Brandy wondered how her Mom got so screwed up.

With that finished, Brandy returned to her major thought for the day. Having sex with Buck at three months wasn't going to be a problem. She didn't feel sick, like everyone said she would. She felt healthy, perfectly fine, happy, and eager to keep fucking. This horniness went beyond teenage years, budding breasts, spreading hips, pubic hair, and first shaving your legs for boys. She had to have some sex at least twice a day. But, what would happen in her ninth month?

Of course, her doctor okayed sex. Still, Brandy didn't want anything to happen to Pomona. She must figure out a way to allow Buck to fuck her with abandon then.

For a while, the answer eluded her. Then, she found a solution.

Brandy's pride shot through the roof. She figured it out. "Why not let Buck fuck me up my ass?" From what her cheerleader friend said in college, "A woman's asshole can take a bigger dick than her pussy any day."

Brandy never considered her asshole a sexual organ. Apparently, she discovered women have been fucking men with their assholes for centuries. This old form of birth control appealed to her. If only she knew about it in high school. No matter what, she could afford birth control pills now.

Lately, Buck's enthusiasm ran the lines of eating dinner between his wife's pregnant, puffy pussy lips. Brandy practically swooned on her burlap chair thinking about Buck's wicked tongue. He dived between her legs looking for clams every other day.

Brandy made sure when Buck got home his meal is all ready for him, warm and juicy, between her legs. "This side dish warms me up for fucking my butt, Buck." Buck chomped right down on Brandy, spreading her meaty pussy. He rolled her inner labia between his thick black lips. The baby was pressing down on her sex.

Her clit seems to perpetually be hard and want to come out and play. He French kisses her soaking pussy. Buck spends a considerable amount of careful time eating Brandy's slot and letting her juices run down to her asshole.

Brandy figured all she had to do is redirect Buck's tongue to her asshole. Then her sex oils and his slippery saliva should make her asshole widen up and take his thick, eight and half-inch cock.

We'll both just have to learn anal sex together. Buck never tried anal sex with Joycelynn. She made it clear she didn't do any sex except dick to pussy on a Saturday night, when they got married six years ago.

Brandy secretly bought anal porno tapes. She watched them while Buck worked. Brandy loved the fact that Buck wanted to make her happy. How calm and laid back he viewed their relationship. He openly courted her ideas about marriage. He wanted, in every way, to make her happy. This was the first time a man even considered thinking about her first, and his needs second. Brandy did not think his job made him this way. She felt sure there were stupid, jerk management consultants out in the world, giving women the short shaft. Buck treated her like...he treated her like a friend. They laughed in bed. Brandy sucked on a fresh banana every week, to keep Buck's robust cock ready for her sassy pussy.

Watching those huge, black men put their dark meat in those white girls' little tiny, star-wrinkled hole caused many thoughts to cruise through Brandy's mind. What if Buck only wanted anal sex from now on? What if Buck refused to have anal sex? What if she hated anal sex? For her, giving up pussy to penis loving was unthinkable. She'd fuck daily to get her pussy to penis penetration.

Watching those anal sex tapes started doing a number on her clit. Soon, Brandy began to realize how precious her asshole was to some men. From her doggy style position, even Akbar seemed to hesitate and wanted to stick his pole up her ass. She wasn't ready then. Brandy studied the women's faces taking hot meat up their ass. They breathe in and out in a certain way. The women always looked back to make sure their man went slowly. They lubed up his penis before, using what looked like KY jelly.

Only when his delicious, chocolate candy bar lodged way deep inside her ass, did the women begin to move and undulate. Pain eventually turned to pleasure. Pleasure turned to ecstasy and ecstasy into sticky hot sperm spurted up their buttholes. Would Buck respect her after anal sex?

Buck accepted her sweating, making ugly faces as her orgasms approached. He even licked up her cream pie out of her pussy after banging her cunt to orgasms. She kept watching one anal DVD after another, until finally, she orgasmed using a black vibrator up her star-winkled hole.

Brandy met Buck at the door, in her red flower and white background sundress. Sundresses doubled as maternity wear for a while. Buck loved sundresses, too. She wore no panties under the breezy cloth. In fact, when she stood by the patio window, as inevitably she retrieved things from the refrigerator or put things into the sink, she blocked the evening sun. Buck got an entertainingly different view of his wife's different charms. She clicked his cell phone off. Brandy pushed him from behind, her small white hands on his back, into the kitchen. She guided him onto one of the burlap stools. Then, she brought out his steak, potatoes and Caesar salad. Each time moving in front of the patio window and sunlight, she placed his food before him. He was her prince and she loved him. She reversed the moves, going to the white kitchen cabinet to obtain a glass goblet, then on to the refrigerator for the chilled wine. He drank wine on special occasions. She didn't talk much, only looked at him lovingly and considered how lucky she was.

Only a little wine remained in his glass. He chewed the last of his food calmly, like he prepared for sex. Nothing ever got Buck overly excited. He remained a capable and stable guy. Brandy sat on the burlap stool at the kitchen table, with her husband. She threw one of her legs across his.

"What's the surprise, Brandy?"

"I'm the surprise," Brandy playfully replied. "It's just you and me tonight. No conversations with Joycelynn about Tawnequa, or whooping it up with your card buddies."

Brandy watched, as Buck rubbed his large thighs. His mustache wickedly twitched like before he went south to munch down on her lily-white pussy.

"Let me think. Guess!"

"You'll never figure it out even if you had a million question long management checklist."

Buck thought of all kinds of kinky stuff to do. Fucking outside in the pool. Brandy said no, but they needed to try that, she thought. He confessed it as his favorite fantasy. Doing the nasty thing before a crowd of people. Brandy said, "Yuck" to this suggestion simply to keep Buck's mind off balance and on her needs. She knew how to be a bitch in the bedroom.

"Bubble bath," Brandy finally tossed out.

"Bubble bath's not kinky!"

"You ever do a bubble bath, Buck?"

Brandy knew she had him. A grown man having a bubble bath wasn't manly, unless his wife gave him one. Brandy wanted to give Buck things, sexual acts he never experienced. She was determined to move up his ladder of past girlfriends, until she was number one.

"I don't normally do bubble baths."

"Okay! Up, Mister." Brandy pulled on his thick arms, his wrist thick as beer cans. She started undressing him. His shirt flew to the floor, as Brandy playfully pinched his black nipples. She rubbed her hand all over his hairless chest, like a washcloth.

Buck rose from the burlap chair and her hands fluttered, like a hummingbird, all over the buckles and buttons, until his huge balls dangled free. Until his thick, long drill-dick hung around, like it needed some attention. She grabbed his dick, after helping him step his feet out of his brown dress pants. Brandy dragged him into their full bathroom. The white tub already filled with hot steamy water.

༺༄༻

Brandy made him step inside the tub first. His six-foot body almost made the water overflow onto the white and blue check tiled floor. Brandy laughed and Buck giggled. He looked helpless under her control, waiting for his bubble bath.

Brandy seductively took a thick, yellow sponge and drenched his entire shoulder muscles and back. She watched the water make his black skin blacker and her white hand whiter. She squeezed water down his back and chest. She rubbed softly and ran her hand across his chest, holding the sponge under his arms, then sides. She reached down his belly and grabbed his hard-on. She squeezed. Pre-cum poured out, into the hot sudsy water. Then, Brandy stood back and slowly raised her sundress over her head, careful not to mess up her short, ash-blonde hair.

Her blue eyes sparkled. Her daring eyes shot flames of desire to his waiting, calm brown eyes. Then, she ran her open hand lightly down between her tits and over her belly jewelry and swooped down between her legs. She raised her hand up and licked her juices. "I think we're ready for that bubble bath."

Brandy stepped into the hot, sudsy water, her crotch practically brushing Buck's black nose. His nostrils flared, when he caught her sensuous, sexy scent. Brandy had turned around facing away from Buck and sat right down, on his hard splashing, bobbling cock.

Brandy proceeded to wash Buck's legs. She washed his thighs and used Buck's large, strong hands to wash her own thighs. She put the sponge in his hand

and directed him where to wash her white body. Her white skin made Buck seem like a shadow. Buck's hands trembled. He loved leaning over his wife's small shoulders and neck, ogling her breasts from this strange position and washing her naked body. His cock pushed against the swollen lips of her sex. He felt Brandy's pussy squeezing back. Brandy washed Buck's arms. She flipped around, like a slippery dolphin, and faced Buck. She leaned her belly on his hard cock. She slithered up and kissed him on his African ancestor lips. Her white, round breasts washed his black chest. Her eyes stared openly, without thinking as she made her belly careen left and right over his turgid tool.

"Wash my ass, Buck?"

He laughed. He always wanted to shamelessly, playfully, caress her soft white cheeks. His eyes opened wider. She leaned into him and allowed him to wash her lower back and ass, between her ass cheeks.

"Wash my lower legs, Buck."

He, again, followed suit, as Brandy slid higher to give him a deep reach between her cheeks. Meanwhile, her pussy mound and clit kissed Buck's arrowhead black cock. Buck trembled, as Brandy wiggled her butt cheeks. "Get in there good, Buck," she whispered and cooed in a naughty voice. Buck responded by swiping the sponge all up and down her ass cheeks. Brandy rewarded him by rising higher and allowing his cock to nestle between her pussy lips, on her piss hole, near her cunt opening.

Buck washed her asshole. Then, he dropped the sponge in the water and used the nearby soap to wash inside her asshole. "He's got the idea," Brandy said to herself. Buck's hands dipped between her cheeks again and again and deep inside her asshole. Brandy's asshole opened slowly, wider and wider, to his massive fingers. First one, slippery one, then two. Finally, Brandy stood up and turned around slowly. She whispered, as she wiggled her slippery sudsy asshole. "Here is the surprise, Buck."

She bent over. Brandy's star-winkled asshole swayed inches from Buck's face. "When I'm nine months pregnant, this is how we're going to make love." she wiggled her ass. "Stand up Buck."

Buck stood up and his drill-pole linked up evenly with Brandy's dick-hungry bunghole. Brandy reached onto the side of the white tub, under the shower curtain. "Use this. Lube up your cock and no skimping on the gel. There's plenty more where that came from."

Buck did as Brandy wanted. He wanted to push himself into her now. Something was loosening up in Buck. He normally stayed calm, but Brandy noticed him wanting to rush things. "Easy boy," Brandy cautioned. "You're going to go all the way down my gripping, shiny asshole."

Buck's dick now dripped KY jelly.

"Now take the tube, place it on my asshole, and squeeze the tube hard."

Buck placed the tube at the beginning of her star-designed ass opening and squirted half the tube up Brandy's ass. "Ahhhh, that feels good and cool." She squeezed some out to assure Buck he put a lot in. "Scoop that up and put it back in my bunghole, with your fingers, Buck."

Buck did. His fingers were now all messy with jell. "You're ready and my asshole sure is ready, Buck. Fuck me!"

Buck's large hands grabbed either side of her modest ass cheeks. He looked down at her slender thighs and those thick calves in between his strong black calves. He pushed his soft, but determined, cock helmet inside and slipped in. "Damn, this is easier than I thought," Buck said enthusiastically.

"Keep going, Big Boy," cooed Brandy, looking over her white shoulders. Her blue eyes dripped sensual sex appeal. The dimple in her chin wet with water.

Buck pushed harder and he met her resistance. "Damn, you're tight."

"We're not ready to rock and roll, yet,

baby, until you pass my virgin gate."

"Virgin gate."

"Every girl has three gates. She's a virgin three times. Her pussy, her mouth's gag reflex and her asshole shutter." Secretly, Brandy felt more pain than pleasure. She almost wanted to stop. But, more than the pain, she wanted to give Buck something to make him feel better. She wanted the pleasure to begin. She kept fucking and bucking against her husband.

Buck's pride shot through the roof. He had taken two of Brandy's virgin gates. Now, his fuck monster knocked at the door of her last gate of resistance. Buck pushed slowly.

"That's it, baby. Push slowly. Oh, that burns, but it feels good."

"I'm not hurting you?"

"I wouldn't be a virgin if it didn't hurt, Buck." Brandy winches and lunged back on Buck's hard body. She felt her shutter opening up slowly, and the slippery lube going down, deeper into her body. "Oh yes, Buck. Slow and easy, but keep pushing." Suddenly, Brandy yelled out, "Yessssss!"

"I felt it too."

Brandy wanted Buck to do the honors, "Fuck my asshole with abandon. Don't hold back."

Buck, for the first time, let go. Something animal came out in him. He pushed hard and sank deeper inside Brandy's body than ever before. The lube on his dick caressed his length. His black veins felt every tight inch of Brandy's muscles tightening and holding him in when he tried to pull out. He went faster in and out. He pushed in and her ass hole burned the length of his drilling black toy. He wanted to shoot off right away, but Brandy reached under between her legs, grabbed his nuts, and pulled hard.

"Thanks, Brandy. I was a goner."

"I want this to last, Buck."

Buck began pounding the babysitter's white asshole faster. The lube began to fly out, off his dick and out of her asshole, in wet flicks, like sparks. He grabbed her cheeks and pushed against her so hard, Brandy had to raise her hand and brace against the front of the bathroom tub. Her knees and Buck's knees gripped the rubber mat and they fucked fast and furious. They fucked hard. Buck emotionally let go and realized he liked ass fucking. "I like this, Brandy. This is the best surprise you've ever given me."

"I know, baby." Brandy cooed. They pushed forward and backwards, at opposite times, until Buck couldn't stand it anymore. Brandy had to brace the front of the bathtub with both hands, as Buck's hands grabbed around her belly and hips and fucked her, until they both came and slipped into the water.

After five minutes of relaxing, they stood up and Brandy released the water. She turned the shower hose on Buck and began to wash his cock off. Then, she washed his body. Then, Buck turned the water hose on her white body and washed her ass and body, too.

Brandy was satisfied and didn't know what else she could give Buck. "I've given you my virgin pussy and my virgin asshole. What else is there, Buck?"

"Your virgin mouth."

Buck's confidence showed. "Didn't I push you past my gag reflex last week?"

"I always wanted to grab a white woman's head and force it onto my huge black cock."

"Like in the porn movies," Brandy jumped up, into Buck's naked arms. "Well let's go, Buck. You're the man."

Buck, naked as the day born, carried Brandy like his trophy wife, into their bedroom. He sat her down on the bed, the same bed five other black buddies of his fucked her to sleep. Now, it was his turn to be master and provider of her greatest pleasure. "We can do that, baby, but let's savor this experience today, tonight," Buck grumbled.

But Brandy insisted. "You don't want everything in one night. I have to dole it out a bit at a time, or you'll be bored."

"No man can be bored with you."

"I'm glad to hear that, Buck." Brandy hugged Buck. "I didn't forget you have a birthday coming up in two months. I'll be five months preggo then, and I have another surprise for you."

Buck smiled and hugged his wife. They spent the next two hours just snuggling, kissing, hugging and smooching, like Brandy liked to do, when she was younger and inexperienced.

4 BRANDY'S BACHELORETTE-
MATERNITY PARTY

Brandy rested. Her head lay on the concrete outside the swimming pool water. The swimming pool water lapped at her gorgeous, 30B-27-35 frame. Her 30B, round tits rising and falling gently under her triangle red swim top. Her matching swim pants barely covered her four-month baby bump below the water line. She completed her twenty laps for the day. Neither her baby bump, nor her child's growing processes, would ruin her slender figure. Brandy playfully allowed her gorgeous, white-skin body to float up horizontal to the water's surface. Then, she kicked her pretty peds in the pool water. Her ivory limbs broke the light blue water surface. For Buck, she painted her toenails burgundy red. He remembered white film actresses with red painted toenails. Brandy smiled. His foot fetish knew little bounds. She had much to learn about how much he loved her pretty peds and her German thick calves. "You have mountain climbing calves, Brandy." He kissed her toes, feet, and calves. "I totally love you, Babysitter Girl."

Babysitter Girl became his new nickname for her. They reminisced Saturday night, after cuddling, kissing, and hugging, how five months ago they met. Refocusing, Brandy tried hard to remember which films these might have been while switching her feet. Using her left foot, she let her body float horizontal to the aquamarine waterline and flicked the water. Waves moved out in smaller, larger and big circles, traveling down the length of their pool. Such a small thing as pretty peds brought them together. Three other white girls failed to realize this sexual power in their possession. Feet. Who would have guessed? She giggled. "Now, was it Pretty Woman? Maybe, Truth or Dare?" Brandy contemplated. She needed to find this film for Buck. Brandy tried a second approach from an actress-to-film analysis. However, she wasn't a big fan of films, except the Matrix Triology, and didn't know the actresses filmography. Buck left Sunday morning. It was now Monday morning. He didn't see her new, lovely, toenail paint. "It'll be a surprise for him, when he returns," Brandy mused.

Brandy's gapping asshole contracted from Bucks enormous length during their bubble bath fuck. His thick tongue humped her asshole a day later, to shower her in appreciation. Brandy walked out of the pool and flicked her short, ash-blonde straight hair backwards. She ran a towel over her hair and presto. She looked pretty and presentable. She dried off on the patio. She sauntered through the kitchen and grabbed an apple off the black and white granite table. No banana sucking activities today. She had business to attend to in the living room. On the coffee table lay her writing paper and pen. "Time for another Mom letter." Brandy figured her mom received the other two letters... In shock, anyway. Concluding, yes, her mom received them. Brandy lifted her pen:

Monday, July 18, 2011
Dear Mom,
I gave up my asshole to my black lover, Buck, last month. I wanted to thank you for passing on your gorgeous white skin and sensuous, "mountain climbing," calves. Buck loves them, and me, totally. I mean, I

really shouldn't say that. The Goddess gave this gorgeous white skin and these sexy calves to me. Anyway, I remember what you said, 'a black guy only loves me for what was between my legs.' So, I figured I'd better diversify. "Diversify: to put one's eggs in more than one pot," Mom. Just so you know, I learned that term from Buck, too. I learned from Buck, of all people, that a woman has Three Virgin Gates: her Pussy Gate, her Asshole Gate and her Mouth Gagging Reflex Gate."

I'm more valuable than I realized. My highest pleasure is to be Buck's Princess of Pleasure. I have more than one thing between my legs that all black men desperately want to get at, or "hit," as rap videos and songs say. I'm not a big fan of rap, unless the music beat is strong and the words are romantic and loving. Now, this ass fucking hurts like a thousand old-fashioned flu shots, all at once, in my ass. My "Ring of Fire" burnt my nerves and I almost wanted to crawl away from Buck's masterful eight and a half-inch black pussy destroyer. We used a lot of KY lube up my tight butthole and it still hurt. Then, the pain gave away and the pleasure came. More pain vanished and more pleasure vied for my attention. Buck said I had unlocked his heart. He wanted to bottle my nearness for his out-of-town trip to Cancun, Mexico. I love Buck. Finally, all I felt was *this exquisite pressure and tightness that consumed my mind and made me want to fuck Buck harder and faster, Mom. I don't know what came over me. I couldn't squeeze Buck that tight with my pussy muscles. I don't know if I'd let any man but Buck fuck me up the ass. His love for me made it all worth it. His love got me over the threshold of discomfort, to the desires of copulation delight. He enjoyed my fantasies of a mutual bubble bath. That, alone, would have made me ass fuck Buck. Yes, Mom, a black, muscular man can enjoy a hot bubble bath with his wife. Provided she presented it in a romantic light.*

I ran the bath, fed him a big steak meal with little red wine, and we went off to our bubble bath. After he took my second virgin asshole gate, my ring of fire, we showered off and went to bed. And guess what we did next? Nothing as terrible as you're probably thinking, with your warped, prejudiced mindset. We cuddled. We hugged. We kissed. We exchanged tender words of love. Then, we repeated the four things, in as many different combination orders as we could discover.

See Mom, Buck loved me, or he wouldn't have cuddled at all. He just would have went to sleep, or clicked on a basketball game, or something. Men can change. They need changing and a special, sex free, woman brings it about. She's got to forget all that nonsense about being either a whore or a Madonna and be both, at the same time.

I'm writing to let you know, Mom, I'm still your white daughter who loves black sausage between her muffin labia lips. Thanks for driving me into the black hands of Buck, because of all your prejudiced worrying and accusing me of already fucking black boys, when I was in middle school. If you had waited until high school, Mom, I wouldn't be so addicted to black men's drill staff, slick fuck pricks. Now, it's too late.

Your loving alabaster daughter who loves fucking black men,

Signed, Brandy the Babysitter

Brandy took a long, hot bath, slipped on her black maternity dress with black casual pumps, and drove over to Heidi's place. Black made her skin seem practically florescence-white. She never wanted a tan, like many white girls.

"This is going to be one heck of a party, from all the cars out front," Brandy said, walking up the sidewalk. She didn't have time to ring the doorbell, when Heidi opened the door, dressed in a slinky white, almost see-thru, negligee.

"Get in here, Bachelorette of Honor,"

Heidi said, as she yanked Brandy's arm.

Brandy felt her growing mommy boobs rub up against the naked, swinging, huge D cup breasts of golden skin Heidi's. "You expected the UPS man, I bet."

Heidi directed her into the spacious living room with three large blue, red, and beige cloth couches. "I've done the UPS man." She winked. "The FedEx man is next."

"We're going to have a fuckfest good time," said a cheerful young girl, sitting on a blue couch, who pushed her large tan tits together, under her hot pink top.

"That's Leela. Leela brings the party with her."

"The girl walking around bottomless, in the too short Hooter's T-shirt, is Margery." Heidi bellowed. "Say hi, wannabe hooter girl!"

Margery's tits couldn't be more than a teacup full.

"It's obvious why she's bottomless," Brandy said, feeling a little over dressed. "Am I overdressed?"

Heidi pulled up her black maternity dress, to her lacy purple demi-bra. "Hey girls, Upritsa," Heidi pointed to the slim blonde in the short blue skirt, pink printed top, and, "Christiana, she's the emu girl, with the long black hair. Stop kissing on Eliza, Zaahira. Is the Matron of Honor overdressed?"

"Heck no," said Upritsa.

"Yeah, her hair is too long," said emu Christiana. Everyone laughed.

Eliza and Zaahira blew Brandy a kiss.

"That means you're okay with the lesbian couple for the night."

"Actual lesbians?"

"Most girls like the softer sex. No birth control responsibilities," Heidi replied and laughed.

"You'll get used to it."

"You don't expect me to..."

"No. I'm an expert in remembering names." She waved Russian Elizaveeta over, "Come say hi, you Russian Princess."

Elizaveeta said something in Russian, and Heidi laughed. "She says you would make a good Chekov heroine."

"I like the story where the guy gets kissed anonymously, by mistake, and believes he's a hero."

"Ahh yes! That was a good one. Poor fellow realized it was all a mistake at the end."

"But the woman had a good time, though."

Heidi raised her eyebrow at Elizaveeta, "She's a gambler." Heidi dragged Brandy towards the couch. "Move over Amelina."

Brandy offered, "I love your long brunette hair and freckles."

"Amelina's specialty is to hold two huge fuck-rods in each hand."

"I've never done that!" Brandy blurted out.

"Perhaps tonight," Amelina said. "After me." Then, the freckled girl laughed.

As Brandy sat down, Quela, who looked like a high fashion Asian model, introduced herself and shook her hand. Hely laid over another beige couch, her legs on the backrest, practicing receiving a blowjob upside down using her black dildo. Ferdina drank some white bubbly wine from a tube glass. She had long, black curly ringlets down her back. Margit had shoulder length curly hair and looked like a freshmen in college. She sat on the couch cross-legged, in her pretty horizontal blue, pink, and white striped panties and pink top. Margit stirred up a desire in Brandy to kiss her. Heidi pointed out Sibbe, dancing to the Cindy Lauper's, "Girls Just Wanna Have Fun." Sibbe seemed as sophisticated as Heidi did. Then there was Gyszel, who looked as if she gave several blowjobs before coming to the party. Her face had a sheen of good sweat. Hanna-Maria wore a cute polka-dot dress that came to her mid-thigh. Brandy saw she had a tattoo of a cock moving inside a pussy on her upper thigh.

"I'll never remember all the names, Heidi."

"Doesn't matter, because..." She reached inside her negligee pocket and looked at her cell phone. The Hot Chocolate Boys of Summer have arrived, women!"

"Whoooooooooooohaoooooo! Yessss! Finalllllly... Some black cock for this white puss!"

"White girls love to fuck black fire hoses," Amelina said.

The doorbell rang. Five handsome black gentlemen came through, into the living room, wearing tuxedos. They seemed more like concert pianists than male strippers. They looked sexy. They placed their CD player on the long coffee table, full of condoms, lubricants, and sex toys. Each guy had a baldhead. Three had mustaches. One had a gold earring in his ear.

Said Tate, "Boys, we struck pay dirt, now. Not one ugly white broad in da house."

All the women blushed and ogled the men up and down, shamelessly.

"Hey Luke, will you look at the con-da-ments." Skylar had a big voice and no mustache.

Luke replied. "Glad you girls didn't start without us."

"I did," Hely said, still lying over the couch backwards, with the black dildo in her mouth.

"Take care of the lady, Wick," said Luke

Wick went over and gently removed the

dildo from her mouth and unzipped his pants. Hely's eyes opened wide, "A real, live, black barber pole." Wick's penis weighed more than a pound of sugar and Hely needed two hands to surround it and slide it into her mouth. Her throat was larger than her hand width, because Wick's humongous tool kept going down and down, until his nut sacks rested on Hely's nose.

"That's fucking amaz-ing," Brandy said. Brandy realized she needed to learn a thing or two from Hely. "I might try using that position with Buck, when he returns."

"Stop showing off, Hely. The boys need their energy to dance."

Brandy hesitated, "I don't know if I want to fuck anyone, Heidi."

"Hot Chocolate Boys of Summer will dance around. All the other girls can fuck them in your place. Virtual fucking, through the other fifteen women."

"Hot Chocolate Boys," Heidi pointed to Brandy. "This cute young puss over here is the belated Bachelorette."

"I'll say," Luke boasted, "That baby bumps well on its way to stopping traffic."

Brandy blushed and didn't know if Luke gave her a compliment, a snide remark, a congratulations, or a come on. "My husband is black!"

"OoooohhHHHHHHHHHH!" all the Hot Chocolate Boys said.

"We're at least four months late, Luke," said Ray.

Christiana, the emu girl replied, "I want an attentive black man, Ray. If you know how many months a girl is..."

Skylar said, "Ray's got a girlfriend, Ray's got a girlfriend."

Ray seemed unsure of how to respond. "Brandy's first. Then, I'll come visit you, personally..."

"I'm Christiana," she said, twirling her long black hair around one of her ringless fingers.

Heidi whispered something to Brandy. Then, Heidi told the boys to turn up their music.

Luke put on "Smack That." All the girls started gyrating and dancing. Brandy, under Luke's guidance, was placed on her knees on a pink, huge pillow. The Five Hot Chocolate Boys of Summer surrounded her and stood swaying together, arm in arm, around her. "Brandy," Heidi said over the rap music, "Do the honor and unwrap your gifts."

Brandy giggled. "I've never had this many black cocks at one time."

"Let's see some black liquorice!" yelled Sibbe.

Brandy faced Luke and unbuckled his cock. She hefted out his ten-inch black meat, a beer can wide. Luke and the Hot Chocolate Boys still swayed. Luke's pleasure sausage smacked Brandy on either side of her cheeks to the music. The hot scene caused Eliza and Zaahira to start finger fucking each other. Their legs splayed while one lay over the other's open thigh.

Brandy opened Wick's black tux pants next and his penis leaped out into her face, hard as a rock. Now, Brandy held two massive black pieces of meat in both hands.

"How much do they weigh, Brandy?" said Heidi.

"A ton, at least." Everyone laughed.

The boys kept swaying and their pricks began to drool clear pre-cum. Brandy's legs became soaked in her juices in half a minute. She desperately wanted to suck down Luke's monstrosity, since he was their leader, the top dog. She rolled her eyes left to Wick, right to Luke. Then, took the plunge and tried to get Luke's monster meat inside her little mouth. She couldn't. Her happy blue eyes didn't show disappointment. She opened wider. Her chin dimple disappeared. She stuck her tongue out. She managed to get him inside her mouth about three inches, before she gave up and swirled her tongue around his cockhead. She licked passionately under his sensitive side. Then, she turned her head to Wick's smaller prick, only seven inches and thinner. She swallowed him down her throat like a real pro.

Everyone applauded. Brandy felt better. She didn't want to imagine Luke grabbing the back of her ash-blonde head and forcing that throat choker of a penis down her small mouth. She unwrapped Skylar next. He was big as Buck. She managed to slurp him down using her tongue as a wedge. She rolled her hips as she moved, and crawled from black cock to black cock.

"Suck that cock," squealed Margit. The college girl crawled practically between Skylar's thin thighs, just for a better look at Brandy's technique.

Three black penis sausages now dripped in her saliva. Tate's dick burned hot in Brandy's hand and now, she wanted a hot cock up her pussy. Tate reached down and pulled up her black maternity dress as she sucked him off. He held the garment around her tits and started mauling them with his skinny black hands. Brandy looked up. She stopped and let Skylar disrobe her. Only her lacy purple, demi-bra covered her from the eyes of the five Hot Chocolate Boys. Brandy imagined herself on film, again. She moved on to Ray, wearing the earring and embolden. Brandy opened wide and gulped him down, deep past her gag reflex, and jerked her head up and down, the length of his fuck tool.

"Help the Bachelorette Girl out, Ray," Luke ordered.

Brandy knew what he meant. Ray grabbed the back of her short, ash-blonde head and his hands messed up her hair, pulling the straight hair over her ears, as he forced her head faster and faster down the entire span of his smaller cock. Brandy opened wide. Her small mouth kept her tongue flat and simply let Ray pommel her face. Ray fucked her face good, and Brandy began to drool. Finally, Ray raised back and exploded inside her mouth. He held Brandy's pretty round face to his nappy brown groin and rolling nut sacks, until he spent everything inside her. Brandy felt so proud. A few more blowjobs like this, and she'll be sure to satisfy Buck's blowjob fantasy.

Brandy's jaw, tired, and lips completely clear of pink lipstick, needed a break. She got up and announced, "The Boys of Summer are Open for Fucking!" Just as Heidi whispered to her before she got down on her knees. In fact, so many of the fifteen girls were licking their lips, Brandy didn't want to deprive them of blowing the guys. She bet Amelina and Gyszel, Leela, Upritsa, Elizaveeta, Margery and sophisticated Sibbe were all better cocksuckers than she was.

"Now, we can service all you gorgeous white dames," ordered Luke. The circle of men, their pants down to their ankles, moved out. They pushed their fucking pricks straight out, seeking a warm wet place. The women swarmed them. The men ended up in a wobbly circle, as all fifteen girls, from Heidi to Hely, descended on their cocks. Margery dragged Skylar down to the carpet and straddled his face with her slick pale pussy, bubbling with her fuck oils, as tall Hanna-Maria engulfed his cock, all at once, down to the root.

Brandy rested on the couch in her demi-bra, her pink nipples hard. Her 30B, spherical breasts poured over the rims, making her look at least a cup size larger. She splayed her legs, one over the red couch arm rests. She grabbed Heidi's gift, a Rabbit vibrator, and jammed it into her cunt. She fucked herself silly. Her eyes closed for a minute, before opening them, when Heidi pressed the button on the damn toy. "It's the Rabbit that does the trick. Let him tickle your clit." Once Brandy turned the rabbit onto her clit, she shot off, into a wonderful quickie orgasm. Heidi said, "Enjoy the show, Bachelorette Girl. You only get to be a married virgin once."

Brandy humped and squirmed under the voyeuristic excitement of seeing Heidi, Mylle and Hanna-Maria fucking the Hot

Chocolate Boys of Summer. Gyszel's sweaty face made her red hair stick to her forehead, as she squeezed Tate's up curved cock and licked the underside. Sibbe and Margey sucked Wick's nipples, Upritsa, standing, didn't take off her blue skirt and pink top, as she forced Ray's face down on her clit, as he knelt before her. Eliza and Zaahira shared Luke's huge cock, after the other girls finished with him. Long, curly, black haired Ferdina massaged Wick's huge balls and her hand covered the length of his cock, as she continually licked and sucked only the tip of his cock. He threw his head back in agony-pleasure. Amelina waited, until Tate and Skylar were finished. Then, she hefted both black cocks in her hands. Even her freckles seem to smile their delight. East-Asian Quela got behind Hely and stuck her darting tongue down Hely's meaty cunt lips.

After every white girl has taken one, or two (greedy emu, Christiana), sucks on each black cock, the five guys began dancing in the nude to the song "Call Me Maybe." The white girls were trying to get the black guys phone numbers. Brandy kept having a good time pushing her rabbit vibrator up her cooze and watching the black guys gyrate and dance before her. Mylle decided to show off and performed a lap dance on the tallest black guy's lap. Mylle was the shortest white girl there, at five feet three-inches and ninety-eight pounds, but she could take a huge cock up her endlessly deep pussy channel. Heidi let Luke, the leader, grope and feel her up on the red couch, while she sat next to Brandy, describing blow by blow all the hot action around. Brandy's cell phone rang and Brandy searched for it, only to find it under the girls in the 69 position, Eliza and Elizaveeta, under the cushion.

Brandy went into Heidi's plush, all pink, bedroom. A big, red, heart shaped balloon floated over a picture of a black man who looked like a pilot. Her bedroom was surprisingly messy. Brandy sat down, on her half-made bed, and sunk down onto the waves. It took her a while to get use to the waves mushing her sweaty thighs and tangy cunt lips back and forth. "Hi Buck,"

"Hey Brandy. I didn't want you to be alone, tonight."

"I'm good, Honey. Just reading another classic, the Kama Sutra."

Buck's loud laugh did not deter Heidi from sneaking after Brandy. Heidi eased down on the waterbed and started mauling Brandy's milky mama tits. Brandy bit her tongue, "I thought you'd be pleased. I learned..."

"Yes, Babysitter Girl?"

Brandy took a deep breath as Heidi slipped two fingers up her achingly empty coochie-snorcher. "I learned... How to fuck you slow. I meant, suck you slow and..."

"Anything wrong, Brandy?"

"I'm about to have an orgasm, Buck." Brandy let out her orgasms as Heidi forced her fourth finger up her slick cooze. "Buck, we're going to have a lot fun when you get home."

"I'll be there the day after tomorrow, Babysitter Girl." He chuckled. "Have fun masturbating."

"Byyeeeeeeeeeeee... Uuugggghhhhhhh... Buck. I missed..."

Buck hung up. Brandy experienced her first bi-encounter and her ravenous pussy felt Heidi's entire fist moving back and forth inside. "Happy Bachelorette-Maternity Girl, Brandy. I couldn't let you leave without having a real cum gusher."

"I gushed?"

"All that liquid is yours, Brandy."

The clear sex fluid covered six inches of Heidi's hot pink sheet, over her undulating waterbed.

"Oh my..." Brandy realized her virgin days were over. Her pussy virgin gate, butthole virgin gate, mouth-gagging gate, first bi-virgin gate, and her first snatch-gushing gate flood. She was a full fucking woman and she loved every minute of her experiences.

5 BRANDY'S BIRTHDAY SURPRISE PARTY

Brandy held the bed covers up to her neck. The bed's warmth reassured her that Buck's love wrapped around her from miles away. She kept replaying the sexual scenes all during her sleep. Buck giving her that hot ass fuck, during their bubble bath. Buck's first time kissing her pedicured feet. All the compliments she received from Hagen and Rex. Her pussy simmered and Brandy wanted to touch herself, again. Her new Rabbit vibrator lay under the mattress. Her lovely furrow grew sweaty and slick. Of course, Heidi's rocking Bachelorette-Maternity Party. Brandy thought back:

"I'm five months pregnant and fucking like a whore," Brandy the Babysitter mentioned to Heidi, after gushing. "I want to fuck somebody."

"Girl fucks don't count, Brandy."

So Heidi began fucking Brandy with the new Rabbit vibrator. They moved into a sensual 69 on their side, and Brandy tasted her first pussy sandwich. "It's not bad." Brandy said, pleased with herself. "I can get to like this."

After their orgasms, everyone else at the Bachelorette party came in, as if on cue, looking for the "Girl of Honor." Everyone took turns tongue spanking Brandy's puffy pussy lips, holding the baby right behind its sacred walls. Brandy relaxed as her cum slipped out of her hot box several times, as fifteen women and five black, handsome, male strippers gobbled, munched, chowed down, and swiped their pink tongues up and down, on her large inner lips and outer lips. Brandy's pussy almost looked like a cookie, except her inner lips overflowed near the top, by her clit. Brandy came a thousand times and fell asleep, exhausted in her satisfied puddle of sex-oiled mess. She was a woman satisfied.

Brandy ran her hands through her hair, combing it, when she woke at midnight. "I'm going to tell Buck, Heidi."

"How are you ever going to make that up to him?"

"I'm going to give him a birthday

present he will never forget?"

"What is that Brandy?"

"I'm going to give him you!"

Heidi's face flickered surprise, then shocke, and finally, a sense of elation. "I can't wait to be delivered in a body-size, round, three-tiered, pink and black birthday cake, on Buck's thirty-first birthday."

Brandy's round face worried, though, as she crossed her legs in her warm bed. Her dimpled chin even seemed concerned. She reached down and rubbed her five-month baby bump. "I'm going to take care of you, Pomona." She didn't exactly know when to tell Buck what she did at Heidi's party. But they kept no secrets. Brandy didn't like secrets. Her Mom, obviously, held some secrets about black men and black cocks that interfered with their Mom-Daughter relationship. Brandy quickly threw off the covers and went to sit at Buck's office desk. She wore a lilac nightie with no panties. She grabbed his notepad of white paper, white as her skin. In college, she learned an amazing new thing. Human skin is the largest organ of the body. That meant her white, alabaster skin was actually her best asset. Not her round face, small cute lips, or luscious calves and thighs. Touch. She needed to touch Buck more on his black skin, his largest sex organ. It made her laugh. She began writing her Mom.

Sunday, August 7, 2011
Dear Mom,
Your black loving, white-trash daughter whore wanted you to have this $1,000. Don't worry, I'm a whore for my husband, the black man, Buck Henderson, remember. I'm sure you still think poorly of my choices. Yep. I'm a kept woman. A whore. I have sex, got preggo, and have sex. This is why I live in such a nice home. Oh, I cook meals for my loving African-descendant husband, but who counts that! It's basically the last hole, between the lips of my pussy that keeps Buck around at all. Isn't that right, Mom? Let's not fool ourselves. There is no way a man would ever love a woman, except for what was between her legs. He doesn't want a friend, or help mate, or partner to raise a family. All a man wants is a sex slave. It's all socially wrapped, in a nice package of self-justification. Right, Mom?

See, Mom, I disagree! Buck loves me and I am his Princess. He is working hard to provide for Pomona and I. He'll be back from Cancun Mexico by the time you receive this letter. The mail doesn't pick up on Sundays. I still get paid for babysitting his girl, Tawnequa, from his failed first marriage. He pays me for cooking and house cleaning, and all that shit not respected in society. So yeah, Mom, I'm a well paid for Whore.

What I really wanted to tell you, I fucked my first woman last night. She's a businesswoman who runs her own Maternity, Bachelorette and sex toy parties. She made me gush. Gushing... rarely happens to a girl. If the right man is fucking her, she'll gush. She gave me this new Rabbit vibrator. So, take that money and buy one. I'll give you one explosive orgasm. The release will probably make you stop hating black men, and being so fucking prejudice against thick black cocks, which you secretly want up your white juice-drenched pussy.

Your loving alabaster daughter who loves fucking black men,

Signed Brandy the Babysitter

Brandy talked on the phone with Heidi and invited her over, during the daytime, to look at the place and figure out how to stage everything. Where the cake will sit? How she will pop out of the cake? How much sex to have with Buck? "Go all the way Heidi. Do whatever you want."

"Really? You only received blowjobs and pussy sucks from the group. Did you tell him that?"

"The less I tell, the naughtier he'll think I was."

"I'd marry a black man like you did, Brandy."

"Maybe I can play match-maker," Brandy winked. "Buck has some black buddies from college. They all have degrees."

"That sounds nice."

"I'll casually mention it to Buck tonight."

Brandy picked up Tawnequa and they went to the zoo. Tawnequa saw the tigers, lions, and the birds. But, she really wanted to see the alligators. "Why do you like the alligators, Tawnequa?" Brandy said, as they walked to the alligator pit.

"Because they have tough skin."

"Humans have tough skin, too."

Tawnequa laughed.

"Your tough skin is your mind, Tawnequa."

"Yeah, I wish I had a sister."

Brandy placed Tawnequa's hand on her five-month baby bump. "Your little sister is on her way."

"You and Daddy having a baby?"

"Yes, it's Buck's baby growing in my belly."

"I can't wait to see her."

"Neither can I."

Brandy took Tawnequa home and, when Buck arrived home from work, they all played "Go Fish." Brandy loved to cook for the two of them. She was beginning to waddle. She could hardly see her feet now. In fact, her sundresses didn't fit anymore. She relied on her maternity wear.

After Buck put Tawnequa to bed, she and Buck talked. Brandy wore her favorite purple crotchless panties and cotton graphic, black sleep-shirt. Buck's classical music played. It was a collection of Hayden's symphonies. He was trying to memorize the entire set. Brandy playfully put her soft white hands over both of his ears. "Buck, block out Hayden for a second. I want to tell you something."

"What is it, Babysitter Girl?"

"If I'm going to return to the University next year, I need to go to night school."

"Night school!"

"How else can I take care of Pomona?"

"You want me to hire another babysitter?"

Brandy thought about that for a nano second. "I'm going to postpone my education, until Pomona can attend school a full day."

Buck listened to Hayden's twelfth symphony, beginning to play. "Easing into negotiations, by saying something outrageous. Knowing I would say no, so you can say something even worse."

"I'm not trying to manipulate you." Brandy almost had tears in her eyes. "I want to finish school."

"It's difficult." Buck said calmly. "We

will work something out."

"I'm not afraid of school," Brandy scolded Buck for thinking that. Brandy put down English Norton's Anthology. "I can get a syllabus for my Nanny/Nursing degree and study on my own. Then, when I go back..."

"Brandy the knowledge will change. New procedures and developments."

"How do you suggest I finish school?"

"Finish school online."

"Online." Brandy's smile widened. Her dimpled chin grew a bit, as her cute small lips opened to kiss Buck on his cheeks and lips.

"Don't give me one of those friendship kisses." Buck joked. "We're so way beyond friendship, now."

"I love you, Buck."

"You're going to finish school."

"I want you to teach me Management Consulting."

He didn't think of that. "Is this the surprise?"

"No, honey." She squeezed his cock, under his dark blue robe. "Your dick will know when the surprise comes."

He shut off Hayden's twelfth symphony. He patted the bed covers. "I think you have the mindset for business."

"Teach me, Buck."

"Don't I teach you already?"

"Besides fucking!" she chortled.

"I've been teaching you business principles every day."

"I've listened." She stopped. "I want to be more than just a wife. I need to be able to stand on my own, in case something happened to you."

"Like what?"

"You might go to Germany to fuck white girls there."

"You're kidding."

Brandy threw herself on top of Buck's body. "I'm kidding." She kissed him hard, as her quick tongue found the back of his mouth. They kissed passionately for a minute. "Your face said everything, Buck. You're not going anywhere. You looked so shocked."

Buck scuffed. "When a man puts all his eggs in one basket, he's got a right to be shocked."

"I'm not going anywhere, Buck."

"Together forever!"

"In love!"

"Let me give you a soothing foot massage, Ms. Together Forever in love." Buck moved to the foot of their bed and sat crossed-legged. His blue robe parted briefly and Brandy peeked at the black cock she'd let into her virgin pussy, forced up her star-wrinkled ass, and pass her mouth gag reflect. She wanted that cock now, but he needed his time to himself, his symphony listening.

Brandy rolled back on her side of the bed. Her sleep-shirt barely dropped below her hips while lying down. She didn't want to arouse him. She began reading her Norton's English Anthology, "Hills Like White Elephants," by Hemingway. "I hate this brief story, Buck."

"Talking out problems is better."

"I know. You can't just know what people are thinking. Hmmmm... I can't see my tootsies."

"I can Brandy." His larger black hands began to kneel, press, and push on her white feet. He adored her white skin. At night, when the lights were out, he still saw Brandy. Whereas he disappeared when the lights stopped shinning. Buck took his time. He started at her toes, pressing the tips. Then, he pulled them gently and twisted them in, with his fingers. He systematically pressed her soft foot flesh down, the length of her white foot. His black hands seemed so much blacker next to Brandy's skin. "The woman who does my pedicure said I'm lucky to have a foot-loving man."

"I remember the first time I saw your feet." He held her foot, letting the warmth of his black hands flow through to her body. "You wore those flowery sandals."

"Sling-backs."

"I wanted you to stand up and kiss me. Rising up on your tip toes."

"I can do that now?"

"The moment has passed." He leaned down and took her baby toe into his mouth. He sucked it and Brandy's pussy began melting.

"Buck," she murmured dolefully. "You're making me wet."

Silence.

"Wet between . . . my . . . legs!"

He sucked her peds slower, "I can suck there, too."

"Buck," she cooed. "I want to savor this massage. You know I weigh more, now."

He sucked her next toe, licking the sides, and kept slowly moving to the largest big toe. Brandy always took care of her feet. When she realized Buck's foot fetish, she always washed her feet before he came home. Before they retired to bed, even before reading, she cleaned her feet. Her foot attentiveness now paid off. Brandy's hands slid up to her round, perfect, tits. "You like my perfectly spherical tits."

Buck raised his loving brown eyes and met Brandy's blue soulful eyes. "I love..." He kissed her big toe on the top. "Every part..." He kissed the tip of her big toe. "This part..." He kissed her big toes right side, then her big toes left side. "Each part of you."

"You never," she pouted, "say anything about my breasts."

"Wait until I find the words to describe them, Babysitter Girl."

His wet tongue sent shivers up from her feet, through her thick German calves, between her sex-flushed white thighs, and straight into her love juice filled cunt-hole.

Brandy pulled her feet out of his erotic hands.

"Hey!"

"I can't let you do that."

"Do what?"

She finally begins to have strong sexual feelings from his attention to her foot. "You're turning me into having a foot fetish, Buck."

"Finally!"

He gently pulled her feet back down to his crossed-legged black thighs. Buck massaged her calves. He lavished attention on her white skin and pulsated the muscles in her legs. He noticed her blue veins. "Brandy, your feet need to be above your head. This helps circulation. It will help you relax as well."

"You'll see my hungry, sexual sweat box, if I do that, Buck"

"Haven't I seen your drooling pussy before? Don't I make your pussy drool?"

"You're my pussy gourmet, Buck."

He placed one foot on each of his shoulders. Buck's eyes fell on her glistening, sweet, sex mound, under her sleep-shirt. He moaned. He murmured. He licked his lips. Buck's hands started wondering around, down her calves and thighs, until his black hands, in their stark blackness, unmistakably moved toward her white sex. Her ivory, gamy, sex waited to be parted. Her glistening, slick groove of desire called for his long, thick, tongue to lick her length.

Brandy closed her eyes and felt the electric feelings rising into her aching tits. "Buck," she started slow and quietly. "I'm going to cum!"

"Don't stop it," Buck kept moving his dark hands as he grazed her sex. He lightly parted her slippery, alabaster, outer lips. Her muffin pussy parted and her love juice ran down its length and pooled at her pussy entrance. She took pleasure in his attentiveness to her arousal. She explored what's next, to make him do to her body. She wanted his thrusting prick in her wet furrow. But where? She grabbed his hands, reaching higher to her inner lips, beautifully curled outside her outer lips. She forced his hands back down and, stopping at her entrance, pushed them into her hungry empty snatch-hole.

Buck got the message and continued to ease his large fingers deeper. Deeper, he went. He even twisted his hands to stimulate all of the ridges of female pleasure muscles inside her proud perfumed cunt. Finally, she came and he withdrew his fingers and licked them.

Brandy finally confessed to all the five Hot Chocolate Boys and fifteen white women who licked her pussy at the maternity party.

"You did more than that, Brandy. I heard all the background noise."

Brandy was shocked. "You're not mad are you? It's like when I fucked your five black college buddies."

"Almost. Except I told you in advance."

Brandy giggled. "Technically, you hinted, but you didn't tell me anything specifically."

"That's because I know you love black cock."

"I know you love white pussy."

"I know what you're planning for my birthday party."

"No you don't. It's a surprise."

"I can take a hint. I'll be surprised."

The mood broke and Buck went back and sat next to Brandy. He began to focus on Hayden's thirteenth symphony.

"Buck, are you mad?"

"Yes, calm mad."

"I didn't fuck anyone."

"Sucking dicks counts."

"Every girl has their sexual bachelorette party."

"You want me to have one, Brandy?" He fluffed his pillow angrily.

"I want you to."
"Do the honors."
"It's all set up, Buck."
"On my birthday."
"She'll be here on your birthday.

Brandy thought, considering Buck rarely got angry, that she did well.

That doorbell, for Brandy, had a distinctive ring today. She had answered the doorbell earlier. She knew it wasn't Buck's birthday cake. Buck sat in the den, watching old black and white movies. He loved those and claimed they made better films then. Brandy catered to his every need with popcorn, hamburgers, French fries, and ice cream. Buck's particularly naughty way of eating ice cream cones, Brandy couldn't stand. His tongue ran around, in a loop. Then, it swooped up the middle of the vanilla coolness. Then, he opened his big lips and chomped up a huge gulp of white sweetness. He did that to her pussy, too. Put his entire mouth over her cunt lips and sucked in. She had to excuse herself to their bedroom, to masturbate using the Rabbit vibrator, before returning to watch the films with him.

She wore her pretty pink maternity dress with the white five bow ties. The clock struck, two in the afternoon, right after the doorbell rang. "Your surprise won't be here until eight o'clock tonight, Buck. Stay right here while I get that."

Brandy opened the door. She signed the electronic shipping docket and had the UPS man move the huge package into the living room. When the UPS man left, Brandy said, "It's a next door neighbor sharing a cup of coffee." Brandy removed the cardboard covering. Before lifting the third tier layer of cake. She whispered, "Heidi."

Heidi made herself very small and crotched near the bottom of the cake. "You said, you'd say Happy 31st Birthday, Buck!"

"Just checking."

Brandy covered the third tier cake back. "Buck! Come help me with this?"

"What?" He stayed glued to the set. "This is a good part."

"Buck!"

Buck came in, wearing his khaki pants and a faded green, men's racketball T-shirt. As he turned the corner into the living room, Brandy yelled, "Happy 31st Birthday, Buck!"

Buck's face flashed bafflement and surprise. "You shouldn't have..."

"Why wait until eight o'clock," Brandy said loudly.

Heidi jumped up, knocking the third tier off the black and pink cake up in the air. She swung her black bra top in her hand, like a stripper on stage, and yelled, "Surprise! Happy Birthday, Buck!"

Brandy wondered what was going on with her. She gave Brandy a WTF look.

Heidi shrugged her shoulders and said, "Help me out of all this sweetness, big black man, because I'm too naughty to stay inside there." Brandy wore a matching black thong, and white high heels.

Buck really liked the delayed nature of the surprise. "You had me going there. I've seen surprise cake parties before. They're predictable."

"Buck!"

"That's why I waited." Heidi handed her black bra to Buck. Buck, placing it into his back pocket and said, "For safe keeping."

Buck and Heidi seemed really into one another. Buck still held Heidi's hand. "Brandy, the music."

Brandy put on "Blah Blah Blah," from Keisha, on their CD player. Heidi started stripping off her clothes (what was left of them) and moving all around Buck. Buck's cock got harder and harder.

"Brandy, is this my surprise?"

"Only if you're surprised?"

"I'm Heidi."

"You're the woman who made Babysitter Girl suck all those black cocks."

Heidi countered with a snide, "She missed your hot tummy tickler when you visited Cancun."

Brandy's jaw dropped. Some how Heidi and Buck entered another world. "Buck, if you want to do Heidi..."

And like that, Buck picked up Heidi and carried her onto the luxurious couch. He laid her down. He dropped to his knees. He removed her black thong. Her golden double D breasts already swayed free. He slipped off her white heels. He wasted no time on her feet. This pleased Brandy, and she sighed in relief. Buck opened Heidi's legs and saw her wetness. He dropped his pants. He pushed his huge cock in. Heidi's mouth opened wide, as she pulled Buck close to her and winked to Brandy. "You're so big, Buck. You could hurt a girl with that monster."

"You surprised me. Now, I surprised you."

This strange fuck mystified Brandy. Buck wasted no time. They fucked like two people on a sinking cruise ship liner. Brandy wondered. "Did I do that by letting Buck fuck my asshole? Is this something he really wants, a golden white girl?" She stood there controlling her expression and playing different rap songs, as Buck fucked Heidi in missionary style, then, doggy style. Then, he sat her on his lap and bounced her high up, in the air, back on his massive cock machine. Finally, they both lay exhausted.

"Happy . . . Birthday," Brandy said, slowly, wondering if Buck was happy.

"He's a fucking stud." Heidi rose up and Brandy went and quickly got her a towel. All of Buck's volcanic cream ran out of her cave-like pussy, down her legs. "I'll just excuse myself to the little girl's room. Heidi left.

Brandy stared at Buck. His black skin shined and was slick in its blackness. She went inside the powder room, where Heidi went instead of the bathroom. "What happened back there, Heidi?"

"I don't know what came over me," She shrugged. "We just hit it off."

"I think," Brandy said, looking at Heidi in the mirror. "He's happy with you."

"You're lucky."

"He's never done me like that,"

"Do you want him to fuck you like a whore?"

"No!" Brandy changed her mind, "Yes." Then, she shook her head. "Did he feel anything for you?"

"Probably not, but that's how these surprise parties go." Heidi finished cleaning up and pulled her black thong back in place. She turned around for Brandy to fasten her bra. "You don't remember those Hot Chocolate Boys?"

"No." Brandy relaxed. "There was sex,

but no feeling."

"That's what you saw today, Brandy." Heidi opened the powder room door.

Brandy exited. Heidi followed.

Heidi said, "Goodbye"' and Buck nodded.

Brandy refused to fuck, or suck, or touch him, in any way for one day after his "Heidi sex," as she called it.

Buck had no clue what was wrong.

6 BRANDY'S FURY

Sitting in the den, topless, wearing only her blue jeans, Brandy was furious. Without her black bella-band, her favorite jeans did not fit, unless she left the button unbutton and zipper opened. Brandy hated when the world didn't make sense. Buck didn't make sense.

She tapped her feet on the red carpet...thinking...thinking...thinking. She changed her position in the recliner. Her fingers tapped the armrest. How could he fuck Heidi and feel nothing for her? How could any man just use a woman's body? His hard body lay on top of Heidi's. His thrill of arousal was obvious for her form. She had a soul. She lived, Heidi did. Brandy moved into their bathroom, her breasts moved outward and inward. She sat down, on the bathtub. Privacy. Peace. She flipped down the toilet lid and sat there, legs spread casually apart. She crossed her arms, under her growing breasts. Her nipples stayed soft. It wasn't easy for Brandy to keep changing places, six months into her pregnancy. But she wanted answers. Walking helped the baby and improved her health.

Maybe, a new perspective loomed on the horizon. Why? Why did Buck show no emotions at all? Writing her Mom always cleared her head. She went back into her bedroom and eased herself behind her office desk. Letters from online colleges, stacked neat in the upper corner, begged for her to open them. A yellow Post-It note from Buck: call Margit about syllabus for nanny/nursing. New, crisp, letters to her detailing how much online universities cost. How many of her university credits transferred. The Modern Dictionary of Business Terminology opened to page 39: Investment Capital. That word didn't describe her anger. Brandy's dimple, on her chin, seemed to drop lower. Her eyes narrowed and became unhappy. Her forehead tried to develop a wrinkle, but she was too young and beautiful to manifest the ugliness she felt for her husband, Buck Henderson.

What word? What word? Ante—a stake

to be paid, to begin participation in business. Almost. Men had no stake to be paid to fuck a woman. He fucked Heidi. Women or girls always paid a stake... their reputation... her questioned commitment. I faked sleeping to avoid that stake. An imaginary light bulb popped over Brandy's ash-blonde head. Speculation— engagement in transaction, or venture, involving risk in hopes of large gains. "That's it." She felt better. Men can have speculation sex, without great risk. Women can't, but do anyway, in the hopes of larger gains... marriage, loyalty. "Yes, speculation."

Brandy turned the new word over on her agile pink tongue, while slowly separating a white sheet of paper from the notepad. She thought, "Time to write Mom."

Thursday, September 8, 2011

Dear Mom,

What do you call a man who fucks a woman without any emotion? A cad? A gigolo? A bandit? You call him a speculator. He fucks women, or girls, on speculation. Speculation—engagement in transaction, or venture, involving risk in hopes of larger gains. The larger gain men get is sexual freedom. The more sex a man has, the more credible, or important, he becomes. Women and girls cannot be speculators. Women and girls do speculate, in the hopes of winning loyalty and marriage of a man or boy, however. I have been engaging in speculation sex. I can honestly say I did it for myself, as much as for Buck, my black husband. So don't go saying what you told me about black male behavior remains true. All men are speculators. All women want to be speculators. The only time a woman can speculate is as a nudist. She can then flaunt her sexual power.

So, I fucked five of Buck's black friends... because I wanted to. Because I wanted to live out my fantasies, and they coincided with his black-white fantasies. I had to act as if I was asleep to avoid the stake. Tomorrow night, though, is Buck's card-playing night, one Friday out of every month. We shall see how the men behave, as I serve their snacks and beverages.

For Buck's thirty-first birthday, I gave him a surprise. He thought he knew what it was. He did not, I assure you, Mom. But, his behavior was abominable, antique, and aristocratic. I gave him Heidi, the nice woman I told you about who runs her own bachelorette-maternity sex toy parties. Heidi hired the Hot Chocolate Boys of Summer to dance for me. I was the "girl of honor." Mom, don't give me that crap about black men. I saw that picture of you and that black man, buried under your religious books. Yes, I'm a snooper. I read the back of the picture. He was your first love. Your

Mom broke you and him up. That's why you hounded me not to date black boys. Speculation attitudes are the problem, not dating black men, or boys.

So, not to lose your train of thought, I gave Buck Heidi, as a surprise, to make up for me sucking off the five Hot Chocolate Boys of Summer. The best I can say is, I had a fucking good time crawling on my bare knees, in my black maternity dress, sucking one African cock after another. One male stripper in the troupe hauled a ten-inch fuck rod, three inches in width. What a fucking hot cock! I only managed to get three inches in my small mouth. That didn't stop me from sucking the other four Hot Chocolate Boys love poles down my throat. So, I felt guilty, like most women and girls, and so I gave Buck Heidi.

In short, out of the birthday cake she jumped, wearing only her golden tan, black thong, and white high heels. Buck took her into his arms and lifted her out of the cake. He placed her on the luxury brown couch and fucked her...just like that! No preliminaries. No chatting. Just laid her down and fucked her brains out. I stood there, hands on five-month prego hips, and watched. He fucked her in several positions. Then, it was over. Just like that. How could he do that, Mom?

Heidi is a person, not a sex doll. She deserves respect. Love. I fucked those black male strippers, but I cared a little for them, personally. Not as much as with Buck, my husband. By the way, I'm writing this topless. I'm wearing the blue jeans I wore when I first fucked Buck that night. I have the button and zipper opened, though. I think a naked body is not lewd. It's beautiful and pure. Nudists don't seem sexual at all. I'm considering being a nudist, although, I'll have to drag Buck to a nudists colony. Anyway, I wanted to share with you my anger over Buck just fucking Heidi without emotion.

Yes, I am being a hypocrite. How can I tell him anything about how I feel, when I fucked his five black college buddies? I did not feel totally heartless as I fucked them. I certainly would not leave Buck for his buddies. That's why I'm angry. There is just no way to discuss this properly.

Your loving alabaster daughter who still loves fucking black men.

Signed Brandy the Babysitter

When he got home, after dinner, Buck read one of several financial papers. He sat, mauling over the small numbered print, as Brandy sat on the bed, in her gray and white-collared sleep shirt. The size was a large, to make it easy to accommodate her six months of pregnancy. She held her belly and listened to an audio book romance novel. She got started on the odd text after seeing Buck's emotionless fuck of Heidi, weeks before. Although she often placed the book on her huge belly, she became concerned. Maybe the girl child might come out with a flat head or something. Audio books also made it easier to ignore Buck while she was angry, too.

"Buck, you fucked Heidi."

Buck turned around slowly, his hand still marking a small column of financial print. "Yes, Babysitter Girl."

"Don't call me that!"

Buck closed the paper. He stared at her. He remained calm. "If this is about me fucking Heidi," he grinned like Rhett Butler, "I remind you that that was your surprise."

"I know, Buck." She stared at her hands, clasped on her six-month belly. "I didn't. I won't. I can't accept…"

"Just say it, Brandy." He crossed his legs, as if he went into negotiation mode. "We married. We care for one another."

"That's it. I don't fuck people without at least caring for them!" Brandy felt relieved she had tossed the bonfire out there. She and Buck would happily jump over and around it, like a mystical witches ritual, or they'd be consumed by its contents.

"You were standing there watching us," Buck placed one hand of his on the other. "What else was I to do? How much affection could I show Heidi in your presence?"

"I should have left the room?"

"I'm not saying it's your fault," Buck went over and flipped through his collection of classical music tapes. "Men basically fuck women like that. We don't get emotionally involved."

"You seemed emotionally involved to me."

His head movement contradicted her statement. "No, Brandy," He pulled out a CD. "It's like a romantic piece of music. You can enjoy it on several levels."

"You just laid her down and fucked her," she tromped into the bathroom hall and brought out a small washcloth. She tossed it into his chest. "There's your loincloth. Be the Tarzan. The caveman in your sex play." Brandy shouted. "Act like some aristocratic, abominable, antique, chauvinistic bastard who rules the world!" She sat back down on the bed.

"Like you sucked those five black male strippers and fucked my five black buddies."

"I'll never love them like you, Buck." She got up, walked over, and stood next to him. He faced her.

"What do you want, Brandy?" He tried to use reason.

"You can't just reason yourself out of this, Buck. We share ourselves and care more for each other."

"I cared for Heidi." He shrugged his massive shoulders, under his black silk robe and pinstriped pajama pants. "We had sex. I was not about to show her emotional sex. I know the difference, as do you, Brandy."

"That is romance." She shouted. "Heidi said you fucked her like she was a whore."

"For Heidi, the romance act equals spontaneity. She gets off on that kind of flash romance," he calmly replied. "For you and me, Brandy, it's on an entirely different level."

"Tomorrow, we shall find out how your black buddies treat me."

"They will show restraint and respect."

"For you, but not for me."

"For you, too."

Brandy walked away, back to the bed, and sat down on the foot of it, staring hard at Buck. "Let's start over again. I don't mind you having sex with Heidi. I mind it being so cold. Of course, with me standing there, it seemed like coldness was the way to go. Perhaps if you apologized to Heidi..."

"I'm not apologizing to Heidi for fucking her brains out, emotionless. You presented her to be my surprise. I expected... to ejaculate inside your small elastic mouth, using my favorite blowjob technique for my surprise." He finally broke his calm. "I wanted you on my birthday, Brandy! I wanted to force your head down, over my cock, like one of those, or all of those, black strippers probably did."

"Only one."

"Brandy," his voice carried intense emotion. "I wasn't your first in that regard."

"His dick doesn't count emotionally. If you say that it counts, then you'll never accept me. I had sex once before you, Buck." Brandy started shouting. "That's the stake all women and girls must pay. If we don't have sex, only with more than one man, we're considered whores. You... men," she spate out, "... can go around having speculation sex with any girl, any number of women. Do you ever see me claiming exclusivity over your past sex experiences?"

Buck reeled. His expression showed episode of their lives irked him. "I have to go get the laundry."

Buck wasn't above getting the laundry. He did it occasionally, to prove to Brandy that he wasn't an aristocrat. "Let's fold these things."

Brandy reluctantly agreed. Her anger began to dissipate. She loved him. Tenderness filled her eyes for him. "You're not buying me off with one night of laundry duties."

"I'm being your modern husband."

She folded one of his dress shirts, "I want a man who treats women with respect."

"Next time Heidi comes over, I will fuck her and treat her just like I do to you," Buck said folding her favorite black skinny jeans.

"No you won't!

"Ah." He grabbed one end of a large black towel she handed him to help her fold. "See! You don't want me showing emotional sex to any girl."

"You really wanted that blowjob from me, Buck?" She said sheepishly.

"Yes."

"But, you guessed that." She moved closer, as they finished folding the black towel. "I wanted to surprise you."

"Every time we have sex you surprise me, Babysitter Girl."

Brandy didn't know what to say. "Where is the sex tape?"

"Secret hiding place."

"Did you make it?"

"Yes," he said, folding a pair of his poker card decorated boxers. Brandy bought them for him on her lingerie, shopping spree. "We're going to play it on a special occasion."

Brandy folded her crotchless panties. "When?"

"Soon."

Brandy moved closer to Buck and tried

to kiss him. She rose up, on her tippy toes, but her belly kept them apart, until Buck leaned over her belly and they kissed passionately.

"Babysitter Girl, only you are my radiant-regal bride."

"Buck, you are my one and only stalwart, sex-stud husband."

Friday night, Brandy's sour mood disappeared, like a sudden rainstorm in a desert, leaving no trace of its existence. Seeing Buck's five black buddies face-to-face, Suhuba, Akbar, Hagen, and Rex made her pussy quiver, searching for something hot to embrace. She wasn't going to fuck anyone tonight. She was six months pregnant, after all. Her sexual pregnancy glow might tempt the black men, but that was their fate for being born male.

Women had so many advantages over men in the sexual departments, Brandy mused, as she laid out chips, sodas, and beers. She turned on the large flat screen to a basketball game. The college season was over. It was a professional basketball player's time for the limelight. She buzzed around, like a Momma hen making sure everything was just right. She even bought a new deck of cards. She wore black jeans, a white bella-band, a green oversized T-shirt, and her white gym shoes with the pink soles. She wasn't about to let the five black men see her pretty burgundy peds.

When they arrived, each one offered a nervous hello. Only Hagen seemed the most relaxed. Probably because he never had any white pussy, he felt secure now. So Brandy understood his near worship of her being. Although, Brandy clearly felt people should worship a Goddess, or God, and not another human being. "Hi, Hagen. I hear you are the youngest," Brandy said, opening the door.

"Yep, the smartest are often the youngest."

"They learn from the older ones," Akbar's deep voice boomed.

"Everyone ready," Buck commanded. "Let's start playing cards. If you want anything, Brandy will get it for you."

Suhuba said, "I want something." He looked at her lovingly.

Brandy waited, pensive, and showed no real emotion. "What is it, Suhuba? Glass of water?"

Akbar jumped in, "He doesn't know what he wants." He laughed at him to scorn.

For once, Akbar's jesting and boasting came at the right time and moment.

"Water would be fine."

"As you can see, Brandy, Suhuba and Akbar don't exactly get along."

"I get along with Akbar."

"I don't like you, Suhuba."

"Stop that nonsense," countered Rex. "They used to go to school together."

"I don't like bullies, Akbar," Brandy cautioned, bringing back Suhuba's water.

Rex said, "You bought us brand new cards, Buck?"

"Brandy's idea."

"I like them," Rex continued.

"Yeah, I had the other decked marked," Akbar said. "That's why I win."

"You win only twenty-percent of the time," Buck countered. Brandy went and sat on Buck's lap, after he dealt out the poker cards. "You boys married, or have girlfriends?"

The men seemed stopped in their tracks.

Rex said, "My girlfriend went back to the west coast."

"She is partying on one of those Hollywood-casting couches." Akbar blurted and laughed.

"She's a real talented actress."

"What about you, Akbar," Brandy said, wrapping her left arm around Buck's broad shoulders.

"My girlfriends never stay." Akbar started to get rowdy, but Buck gave him a look and Akbar calmed down. "I am really an independent man. I love my freedom."

"I like my freedom, too," Hagen said.

"What man doesn't like his freedom," Brandy smiled. What man doesn't like his freedom? "I was lucky to catch Buck."

"You have any other sweet, white girls like yourself, Brandy?" Suhuba said, tossing out a six of hearts.

"Not like me, anyway." She thought, moved closer to her husband, and whispered something into his ear. Buck smiled broadly.

"She can fix you up with some white girls."

Brandy shrugged, "I don't know many black girls."

All four men became more animated and talked at the same time. "Do it!"

"Let 'em come on."

"Set up the party," Akbar's deep voice boomed.

"I have just the girl for you, Akbar."

"Oh yeah!" He scooped up the pot money, as he won the hand. "What's her name?"

"Heidi."

Hagen said, "A nice German girl."

"I do German girls."

All the boys laughed.

Brandy teased them. "German girls are all over the globe, now, anyways."

Buck closed his hands and laid his cards on the table. "Brandy, tell the guys these girls are fast though."

"These girls are fast, boys."

"Fast?"

"They don't mind fucking black men," Buck replied.

A huge roar went up at the table of black men. They laughed and gave each other high fives.

"Set it up, set it up, set it up," All four men yelled in unison.

Buck's four black buddies helped put the card table back in the den, before they left. Buck and Brandy cleared the card table and cleaned it up. "They behaved themselves respectably, Buck," said Brandy, removing the potato chips bowel. Brandy wiped where the bowel was and cleaned the other parts of the table.

"Only because you offered them some more white pussy," Buck replied from the kitchen, washing the cups of coffee.

"Long as they know these white girls deserve respect." Brandy said, pushing each chair.

Buck wrapped the beer and soda cans in a green plastic bag, "Do you really think Akbar and Heidi can hit it off."

"That's a statement, not a question, Buck."

"Heidi's a powerhouse," Buck kissed his wife. They sat down at the card table, all clean.

Brandy sat on his lap.

"Heidi's the Boss of her own business." She hugged Buck. "Akbar would eat up and abuse any other girl. He needs a bossy girl."

Buck laughed.

Brandy told Heidi about her argument with Buck. Heidi agreed to their emotionless sex, but disagreed Buck mistreated her. "At least, Buck didn't go behind your back and try to fuck me. Other men have done that. Upfront sex is the best of all. It was only about sex. Not love."

"Sex leads to love, often enough."

"Here is what I think, Brandy. He wanted you on his birthday."

"That's what he said."

"Men can fuck out of spite, or revenge, just like women."

"You think he fucked you that way, because he was hurt?"

"Every man wants his wife to be only with him."

"I don't buy that old paradigm shit, Heidi. We are not soiled goods, because we fucked once before."

"That's what all men have to understand. Love is the only thing that makes them understand that."

"I agree. Love is the only thing." Brandy said, "Keep in mind, Akbar is really a loud and boastful black man."

"I've slept with his type before," Heidi

said. "Be right back, the FedEx man."

Brandy waited. Then, she heard over the phone, Heidi making sexual sounds and saying, "Stick your huge black package up my tender, small, tight cunthole." Brandy waited. Heidi made other lewd sexual statements, until Brandy realized this was for real. "I guess you'll be a while, Heidi," Brandy said into the phone. "I'll call you later, to set up the party."

So far, Margit, Sebee, Russian Elizveta, Hanna-Maria, and the emu girl, Christiana, agreed to attend the matchmaking party, as Brandy began to call it. They would have a fun time. Brandy realized they'd have a fun time fucking, using their pussies and assholes, while she shopped for food and drinks. I'd better bring lots of condoms and KY jelly, too.

7 BRANDY'S SECOND ANAL ADVENTURE

Brandy had a lot to think about. When she last fucked, or sucked, a black man's horny, stiff cock, she was five months pregnant. Fucking her Rabbit vibrator didn't count. Fucking her new black dildo didn't count either. What would have counted is fucking the FedEx man, who mentioned Heidi's name, when delivering her maternity gift. The card inside the small envelope on the package read, simply:

Dear Brandy,

Thanks for allowing me to perform at your birthday surprise for Buck, your handsome black husband. He gave me a fun-thrilled and guilty-free fuck, which every girl needs every so often. He flung himself on my hot golden body and didn't stop fucking until I came. He made me desire marriage again. I learned from your experience not to give up searching for the right black man to power hump my narrow wet slit for eternity. Thanks again for sharing Buck's big black fuck-sword up my sheath, white cunt. I craved his eight-inch black cock ever since you first mentioned his name.

Your Friend,

Heidi

P.S. Thank you for the written invitation to your matchmaking party. I will be there wet, open, and ready.

Brandy turned the elaborately decorated, beige and burgundy, script card over in her hands. Heidi exuded class. Brandy clasped it to her breasts. The card made her less apprehensive that Heidi planned on stealing Buck. Or that Heidi already had stolen Buck. Her gift was a small book entitled, "How to Let Your Big Man Deep-Throat Fuck Your Face" by a well-known Internet porn star. The porn star's book sold all over the Internet. Funny, Brandy thought, "I never heard of it." Brandy didn't use the Internet that much. Brandy planned to start reading it, after the important letter to her, Mom.

Thursday, October 13, 2011

Dear Mom,

All is well between Buck and I again. You don't think sharing your girlfriend with your husband is a big deal, at first. Feelings of jealousy, rage, insecurities, and betrayal surfaced for me, whereas Buck handled himself like a gentleman. We talked it out, and he refused to show Heidi an emotional fucking, or preliminaries, because he really wanted me for his birthday surprise.

Me! Yes, me, Mom! We folded the laundry together and talked it out. He wanted to fuck my white round face, using that mouth-watering night cock and plum-size nut sacs of his. I thought he'd guess my face-fucked gift. That is why I provided Heidi.

Heidi, for her part, sent me a nice, formal thank you letter, on nice stationary. Not some crappy Internet thank you shit. She said, "Buck made me desire marriage again. I learned from your experience, Brandy, not to give up searching for the right black man to power hump my narrow wet-slit for eternity."

That's why I'm writing, Mom. Enclosed is another $2,000. I am so big. I'm a whale! My belly sticks out and everyone knows I'm pregnant. Everyone knows I fucked someone. Everyone who sees me and Buck, out at a play, or concert, or sporting event, knows that black dude fucked that white pussy. I didn't show much my first three *months. I grew some in the fourth month. I was smaller than most women were at five months. But, I sure caught up with the average woman last month. I want you to come and visit me. Spare no expense. Buy the clothes, shoes, and lingerie you've always wanted. Pedicure your nails and feet, and come join me. We're having a party on the 20th of January 2012 at 6:00 PM. Besides, I'm due the 31st of January 2012, or 3rd of February 2012! I want you there, for my daughter's birth. You can sleep in the den, or we'll put you up in a hotel, if necessary. I know you are receiving these letters, because they don't return, Mom. So, don't give me that shit about you didn't know.*

Your loving alabaster daughter who loves fucking black men.

Signed Brandy the Babysitter

Brandy waddled away from her office desk. In another month, writing there would be impossible. It never occurred to Brandy how pregnant women wrote letters in those olden days. After crawling back into bed, Brandy lay on her side and thought carefully about her Mom, Alice. Brandy wanted her Mom back. If Mom reconnected with her first love, the black guy Leonard, who was now a cargo pilot somewhere, all would be happy, again. From the air pilot's photograph, Brandy realized Alice's Mom broke them up, when

Alice was sixteen and Leonard was eighteen. This made them high school sweethearts. They probably had sex as soon as they turned eighteen. One year later, she was born. That made Leonard Smith thirty-seven now. Alice's Mom died five years ago. She didn't like the fact that Alice was white and Leonard was black. To add to that, Leonard probably had no clue what kind of job he'd have. Whatever the reason, the two of them kept in touch. Alice married John Tuey, a bum trucker who eventually ran off and left the two of them alone.

Brandy never tried to find a missing person before. She knew the Internet and a phone number was enough to start. She got out Buck's iPad and started clicking around. She found a site telling how to find missing persons. First, she needed a full name and a social security number, an occupation, and last location. Zaba search became her first try. Brandy happily found others looking for former lovers and high school sweethearts.

Later that evening, Buck came home from work. "Hey Babysitter Girl, I'm home!"

"Buck! Exciting news," Brandy said, running out of the bedroom in her black bella-band, jeans and no shoes, or socks on. His iPad dangled from her hand. Buck liked what he saw. He practically licked his upper lip. He stared from her nude feet up to her round, pretty face and blue, happy eyes. She came up to him, leaned into his arms and they kissed. He picked her up and sat her down on their living room couch. "Just let me look at you." He shook his head in disbelief. "You are so fucking beautiful."

Brandy played up his lust, by stretching out her legs and pointing her bare feet at the recliner he sat in, to her right. From Buck's perspective, Brandy realized, he focused on the tips of her toes and the polish on top. Luckily for her, pedicures were okay during pregnancy. "No sex tonight, Buck."

"Why?"

"Because I need your help? I'm narrowing down the Leonard Smiths."

"Why do I care about Leonard whatever?" Buck leaned back and took in his wife's gorgeous, spherical boobs. "I want to suck your growing tits. You're already a C-cup." He playfully hopped on the couch, by her side, and tried to grab her heavy breasts. The nipples began to distend and full out her milk glands.

"Stop that!" Brandy said seriously. Her smile narrowed and her blue eyes became unhappy.

"Maybe, if you're good, Buck. We must

reconnect two lost sweethearts, one black and one white."

"Your Mom, Alice?" Buck forgot about the sex. "I know how important this is for you, Brandy... Getting your Mom and her black lover back together..."

"Listen. I've narrowed it down to three Leonard Smiths who are Cargo Pilots."

"Cargo Pilots may be hard to locate, flying every day and all."

Brandy showed him the Google Map. "Look, one in Phoenix, Arizona. I don't think he's the one, because he flies inside the USA. This one, in England, flies only in the USA and England."

Buck watched his wife's intensity. "You've done a lot of work."

"I'll say, I started with fifteen hundred Leonard Smiths that are black, at ten o'clock this morning, after I wrote my Mom."

"You're writing your Mom?" Buck didn't know if he should be apprehensive, or surprised.

"It's a good thing Buck." Brandy flipped the iPad page to a calendar. When we have our match-making party, I expect Mom to be here!"

"Your match-maker orgy."

"You agreed to it the other night."

"I did?" He paused. "Before I knew your Mom was attending."

"We're going to hook up your black

buddies with wives, and those Hot Chocolate Boys, too."

"I might." Brandy joked. "Of course not! I want my Mom to be happy again. We can be happy together."

"Let's say he is in the Philippines..."

"I left a message with the ALPA, Airline Pilot Association."

"Did Leonard call?"

"No, but they gave me his number." Brandy clicked on an email. "I told them their love story. She's white, he's black, and they were too young to marry. He didn't have a job. They were both eighteen. They've been in touch, ten years ago. That's how I had his last location, in Taiwan."

Buck picked up the iPad, clicked around in the Goggle, and zoomed into Street View. "That's where he lives."

They looked at the place.

"Nice street!"

"Does he want to come back here, Brandy?"

"I know he still loves my Mom."

"Why can't he fly in the USA?"

Brandy's face changed to melancholy, "I don't know."

Buck laughed and laughed. "You're crazy fun, Brandy." He put his head down and kissed her belly bulging out over the black bella-band.

"Don't make fun of my maternity

wardrobe." She hissed.

"What is this?"

"Bella-band keeps my pants up." She stood up and turned around. Buck saw her jeans fit just like when he first made love to her. Her flat butt checks narrowed down, into her crack, and made him want to run his hands between her legs. "You don't need to button, or zip up, your pants."

"It's kinda cute."

"Stop interrupting, Buck." Brandy narrowed her blue eyes and focused her thoughts on him. Silently saying, "Listen! Listen, Buck." He received the message and became serious. "I've sent Mom some money over the weeks. I sent her $2,000 just today. I told her we're having a party for the baby and I want her to be here. I'm going to surprise her by..."

"Having Leonard Smith here." Buck thought carefully about this. "You're one diplomat, if you pull this off.

"They are still in love, Buck. Imagine if someone broke you and me up, when we were young. How terrible. The agony of not being able to express their love for one another, for decades, Buck. I couldn't bear it. I now understand why she was angry with me. She didn't want me to end up like her. At first, I thought it was only her prejudice, but I knew it had to be more. When I found this picture, I assumed the date was the beginning. Ten years ago. But, that must've been when they tried to reconnect! Mom struck out against me out of jealousy, fear, and anger." Brandy went into the bedroom and pulled out the old photograph, stolen from her Mom's high school yearbook.

"So, that's the brother."

Brandy saw Buck's face registered a special sympathy. Buck knew his pain. Buck did not want to lose Brandy.

"Isn't he cute?"

"Brandy, you're not thinking of fucking him, too."

"Something about his flight training or hours."

"He'll need a new line of work here."

"He's a Captain. He's in management."

"Okay. Let me know what develops." Buck picked up his wife's feet and put them on his lap. He started massaging her soft, white feet. His hands explored the curves in her slender, tiny feet. He admired the arch and smooth white skin that led to her thick calves. He leaned down and started kissing her feet. "Buck...I really want to make love... through my backdoor tonight."

"Is the front door closed for business?"

They laughed.

"Listen, we'll put your Mom and Leonard in the bedroom by themselves..."

"If they come?"

"They should have privacy." Buck said, rolling his wife's heels under his strong hands. "Did you know that, according to reflexology, certain spots stimulate the sex organs?"

"You fuck-friendly fiend." Brandy pulled her feet up to her knees, as best she could in the tight jeans.

"Let's get these pants off of you."

"Before what?"

"Before you soak them through, because I've been massaging your heels. I know you want my big black dick now."

"Buck, something's come over you, since I let you have my backdoor."

"I'm the same as before."

"You're more demanding." And Brandy reached and squeezed his groin. "And you can't use that old wives' tale about getting less sex, because your wife is pregnant."

"No I can't." He had her jeans around her ankles. She had on white panties with tiny pink roses on. "Is your underwear, bella-band? I don't know all the new changes in your body... Brandy, it's driving me crazy. I have to have you!"

Brandy realized. She understood. This is that moment in every marriage, when a man wants to fuck his wife. She is preoccupied with pregnancy, cleaning the house, and preparing for the baby. Does she let him have her, or deny him? She laid practically nude, the black bella-band around her belly and the top of her panties. Buck's dark hands slowly slid down her heavier, ivory thighs and thicker calves. "They say black men like women heavier and not skinny."

"You better lose any weight you gain, Babysitter Girl."

"I swim every day. I masturbate every morning. Losing the baby weight after my pregnancy will be easy. I dream of being the slender white bitch you always wanted, Buck." She turned over on her hands and knees. "The bella-band will make things sexier for you, Buck. It'll remind you I'm as white as a cloud. You can grab it to hold my hips, too."

Buck took hold of the flexible material and pulled Brandy back toward his face. He hadn't changed his sitting position. Her bulging cunt pressed outward. He was even able to see her love hole, as she knelt. He let his hands feel up her ass cheeks. His hands, scenic tour, went all up and down her legs. "I need to get a pillow to put under your belly. You must have developed two months' worth, in one month."

"I know it." Brandy turned back and smiled. "I'm a gorgeous white cow now. But, I want to feel the weight of my belly, while we're ass fucking."

"As you wish." Buck went to work, licking his fingers and probing his wife's pussy. His foot massage turned on her libido. He slid his large fingers into her outer lips. His fingers were soon covered in slick juices, from her desire. Buck felt her inner lips and pulled gently on them. He pulled them apart and dipped his thumb into her hot, love box. Brandy rewarded him by coating his thumb liberally with her lusty juices. Buck brought his thumb out and dipped them into his young, Babysitter wife's asshole. He soon had no trouble sliding his thumb in and out of her backdoor, rapidly. Brandy moaned and wiggled her ass cheeks. She waddled on her hands and knees. The weight pulled down on her clit. She felt hornier than ever before. Buck's left hand reached under her white legs and playfully slapped one breasts, then the other. Her nipples responded by darkening. Tightening. He kept touching them, rapidly. He swirled his hand around, in a spiral, going out from her nipples to the perfect roundness of her spherical breasts. She moaned and loved it. "Buck, make love to my asshole."

"Your wish is my desire."

Brandy's head rested on the brown leather couch, as she stared between her legs as Buck undressed. His balls seemed like pool balls from her point of view. His dick expressed more fertility, as the veins became more prominent, as he hardened and lengthened. Her juices ran out of her cunt, down her slit grove, and pooled into the hood of her clit. Brandy listened carefully.

Buck positioned himself. He hefted his dick up and down her pussy crack. He pushed two of his fingers inside her wet cooze and slicked up his midnight cock pole. Brandy realized they were going to ass fuck without KY. Could she do it? She willed her asshole to open wider. She relaxed her pussy muscles. Buck's three fingers swirled around and around her pussy. He reached deep inside her cunt, to her G-spot. She didn't realize he knew about her G-spot. He kept fingering her and pressing. Brandy felt a new fire of passion coming from deeper inside her cave-like pussy. She pushed back and rocked forward. Buck pulled out his three fingers and, one by one, slipped them up her asshole.

"Do me, Buck!"

Buck wanted to show his wife that he wasn't squeamish. He raised his hot meat up and nudged the sponge-soft head of his cock to her asshole. The knob slipped in easily and Buck pushed slowly. When he reached her ring of fire, he rocked back, pulled the bella-band up, and slid right over it. Her ring of fire burned for a brief moment, before it gave way. The bella-band put an unusual amount of pressure on her clit. Every time Buck pulled the bella-band, Brandy wanted something up her cunt, or ass, or both. "Is this what you want, Babysitter Girl?"

"Ahhhhhhhh, yes... Fuck my asshole good!"

Buck slapped her flat, wide ass cheeks. He saw the sex flush rush out from her cunt, down her lovely legs and thick calves, before it rushed upward and covered her large belly and full breasts. She turned back over her shoulders and said, "Buck, you're a monster back there."

"You feel so hot and tight, Babysitter Girl." His face turned from skilled technician to someone given over to passion. His eyes closed as Brandy's eyes did, too. They focused on the feeling their hot, wet flesh provided. She rubbed her own tits with one hand, as Buck found her clit in his left hand. They rocked and Brandy couldn't get over the white glow of her flesh against his darkness. She loved Buck using all her heart and body.

Buck wanted to pull her short, ash-blonde hair. Then, he did it. He reached up and grabbed Brandy's hair. Her lovely round face rose backward, and this stretched her tits in a new way. Brandy's horny tit nipples reached for the sky. He pulled the bella-band up and Brandy rose onto her knees, on the luxury brown couch, her seven-month belly sticking out. Brandy accepted Buck's pride in knowing he knocked her up and put her in this sensitive and sensual position. Buck's balls slapped against her ass cheeks and Brandy loved the audible sounds they made. Her sucking asshole grew wetter as her cunt fluids rolled downward, onto the base of Buck's tremendous undulating balls. Brandy's ass muscles felt every vein on top and below his ebony dick. Her ring of fire pushed her higher and higher, up the ladder of lust. Buck's fingers reached under the bella-band and stayed there in position, to stroke her clit button. He stayed on target and pressed, rolled. He pinched. He flicked her clitoris, until Brandy couldn't take it anymore and stars burst behind her mind's eye exploded, as she came in an orgasmic rush.

Buck wasn't done, though. He snaked his fingers down her lily flower's inner lips, drew up more moisture, and attacked her clit again and again. Brandy did not think she could come twice from ass fucking. Buck proved her wrong. He was a maniac. He displayed someone determined and confident about ass fucking and mauling his young, white wife. Brandy yelled, "Take me, you black brute."

Buck obliged his white wife by fucking her faster and faster. He placed her gently back on her hands and knees. Brandy allowed herself to lower her shoulder and Buck went so far in, he had to concentrate on getting back out of her poop chute. He knew lasting longer, after traveling this deep, was impossible. "Brandy, Babysitter Girl, I'm about to shoot my white spunk up your dark channel."

"Stop talking and fuck," Brandy cooed. This one time between them, things seemed reversed to Brandy. Buck, filling her with his white, fertile man-cream and her dark ass chute collapsing, controlling, and pulling that cream deep into her dark asshole.

Finally, they both shuddered, Brandy, the second time, and Buck, his first. Buck pressed down on Brandy's hips. Her shoulder rocked into the brown leather couch and her pussy drooled cum down her legs, as Buck spurt his seed up her worn asshole. Buck paused. He savored his monster tool growing smaller and smaller, shrinking after having its exciting epic journey up her star-wrinkled hole. He quickly went into the bedroom, grabbed a large, white pillow, and placed it under his wife's pregnant belly. She lay comfortably on it. Then, Buck went and got a towel and cleaned them both up. They lay on a sheet and went into a fuck-exhausting sleep.

When Buck and Brandy woke up, they

laughed. His hardening dick tried on its own to get inside her waiting, open, pregnant pussy, as they lay in the spoon position, him behind her. "You want to do it this way, Brandy?"

"Why not, my black-stud?" Brandy, the white Babysitter and black Buck Henderson let nature take its course, as he simply moved one inch and climbed inside her. They found themselves, lock and key, in their intimate embrace, again.

8 BRANDY AND THE NUDIST CAMP

"Hello, I'm trying to return a call to Brandy Hu," Brandy heard the message recording on her cell phone. Brandy lay on her side, in bed, and the cell phone rest on the desk. Brandy waddled, as fast as possible to reach her phone, but the messaged clicked off. She pressed the autoreturn and got no answer. "Damn. I know that was Leonard. Why was he calling me Brandy Hu?" Brandy had begun carrying the cell phone everywhere, after missing the first call from Leonard Smith, in the Philippines. The time difference of eight hours made things difficult by themselves. Then, if there was one toss in his odd hours of cargo flying, 13:40 PM here, it was 1:40

AM in the Philippines, or Australia, or Singapore. Brandy worried her Mom might never find her lost love.

Buck had turned the cell phone off, to get some sleep. He set her alarm to wake up at 6:00 AM. The alarm turned on the phone. She slept right through the alarm. Brandy knew Buck needed his rest. She'd figure a way to connect to Leonard. She had two more months to reach him, before their matchmaking party, on the 20th of January 2012.

Brandy's doctor told her the baby girl's height measured eighteen inches long and she weighed four and a quarter pounds now. She didn't have many varicose veins, because Buck always massaged her feet, calves, and legs. Her doctor congratulated her on having such a wonderful husband. "Oh, you won't believe how wonderful he is, doc. He lets me do everything I want."

"Then, he'll let you wear stockings to prevent varicose veins."

Brandy chirped, "He sure will." Buck didn't particularly like stockings, but when he saw the black stockings on her, how her white, thick legs glowed through those sheer black stockings, he practically forced her wear them. Brandy knew Buck's foot and leg fetish soared now, through the roof.

She casually worked on string, or flute, concerto after another, into her listening day, beside her audiobooks. In Lamaze class, they mentioned that listening to Mozart made babies smarter. Brandy even placed their black deluxe headphones on her big white belly. The music helped her appreciate how nice and kind Buck behaved as a husband. She heard horror stories from some of her Lamaze classmates. She didn't want to think about abandonment. She was determined to give Buck as much attention and sex as he needed. Buck was very unassuming about her sexual needs. He felt she needed sex like him. She needed rest like him. The team pulled each other's weight, and different manners and styles.

Love described their relationship. She spied him loving her with his big brown eyes. He showed his love by using tender words and remaining calm. Even when she had her brief, bout of pregnancy sickness, one week last month, Buck helped her as much as possible. His approval made her gush and her heartbeat a tango web of intermixed emotions. But now, Brandy needed to get out of the house. She went enough places for the baby, true. They both attended a Halloween custom party at the convention center, for business executives and their spouses, yes. Buck dressed up as Maria, a pregnant Antoinette's husband. No one at the crowd missed their interesting twist on the French Revolution. She thought of going as a pregnant Daughter of Dracula, but the blood and pregnancy didn't go well in her mind. Her ghost-white skin made an excellent Marie Antoinette, however. Still, the places she passionately wanted to go with Buck fell into the category of sex, or sexesque. Sex-live theater, or a nudist camp. They went to see a couple of sexual, R-rated movies and Buck played around with her milk-filled tits. He slipped down on his knees and ate her pregnant pussy. His black, curly hair tickled her white thighs, under her wide skirt, as they sat in the back of the darkened theater, but that wasn't enough. She wanted to go somewhere naughty and celebrate their sexuality.

While she marveled at her luck in snagging Buck, and designed better sexual fantasies to play out, he continued to teach her about business. The latest word she learned was balance of trade—difference in value between nation's imports and its exports. She laughed when he mentioned that, because if her body was a nation, she received a balance of imported and exported cocks inside her tight, pink pussy. Brandy thought of how, just a year ago, her pussy barely knew what sex was. Now, her experienced pussy explored some seven black magic wands (if she included the black dildo), one Rabbit rubber wand into her soft peach-middle gate. Her mouth swallowed ten black-licking swords. If she fucked those hot chocolate boys at her matchmaking party, like she planned, that'd make thirteen fuck wands!

Arranging their attendance at the Shore Bluff Nudist Camp in Florida made her cunt tingle. But first, she had to find her Mom's ex. She picked up the phone and dialed again.

"Leonard! This is Brandy Tuey."

"Tuey! Alice!"

As soon as Buck left for work, her attention turned fifty percent of her time finding Leonard, and another fifty percent of her time reading up about a nudist colony down in Florida. Escaping the November chill would do her and Buck some good. She wore Buck's blue robe and her blue bella-band and black cotton panties and stocking. Buck's stocking fetish developed, because he watched and listened to her sexy white legs swish together, as she waddled around the house. She still cooked dinner and breakfast for him. Sometimes, she even wore garter belts. Together, finding Leonard and arranging for the Shore Bluff Nudist Camp kept Brandy excited, like a child at Christmas. Brandy dressed to go out and get the mail. Then, she began calling the airports and making flight arrangements for the 18th of January 2012. First, she booked a flight from the Philippines national airport, back to the states. Then, she reasoned, if it was 1PM in the afternoon here, Leonard should be up at 1AM there. Since he recently called, perhaps he was taking off on a flight and had to turn off his cell. Brandy tried the phone number, again.

"Hello, I am trying to reach Leonard Smith."

"This is Leonard." Such a loud roar of background noise, planes, cars, and buses complicated their communications. "You have to speak up," he said.

Brandy held the phone an inch away, in front of her mouth and shouted, "You don't know me, I'm Alice Tuey's daughter."

"Alice Hu...?"

"Alice Tuey, Tuey... Your old flame."

Silence dominated the other end for minutes. Only the roar of noise filled the cell phone.

"Alice?"

"No," Brandy shouted, "Brandy Tuey, Alice's daughter."

"You have to hurry up. I have a cargo plane to fly."

"Alice Tuey, my Mom wants to see you again, Leonard." Brandy said quickly. "She's single and misses you."

"Alice..."

"Yes, Alice. She's fucking hot, Leonard."

"Alice was one hot white chick back then. She got married."

Brandy had a hard time making out long sentences as all the engines roared. "She's divorced," Brandy lied. On the 20th of January 2012 meet us at this address."

Brandy gave the address. "I'm going... I'm going to text the address to you, Leonard."

"They're calling me to the plane." Leonard's voice sounded faint, as if he were moving into the noise, or wind. "Text me. Bye."

And that was it. Brandy clicked the cell phone and held it to her bare breasts. "Mom and Leonard are going to be together, again!" Brandy couldn't believe her ears. She did it! She texted her address and told Leonard his plane ticket from the Philippines waited for him at the airport on the 18th of January 2012.

Brandy started to write another letter to her Mom. Then stopped. She balled up the paper. I'd better wait until after Thanksgiving. I don't want to shock her. Then, Brandy reconsidered. What if Mom meets someone over the holidays? People are always lonely around Thanksgiving and Christmas. She pulled out another piece of paper.

Monday, November 14, 2011

Dear Mom,

Don't fucking go get a boyfriend or anything! I have someone you need to meet. He's lonely and a really nice guy. He's black and loves to fuck white girls. Mom, I think it's time you buried the hatchet against fucking black men and give in to your lust. That's the only way to conquer it. Once you fuck this black guy, you'll love having sex with black men, again!

I'm making plans to get away to a nudist camp in Florida this month. I'll tell you how it went when I return. Maybe, I'll even have a tan, (sticks finger in mouth, yuck, yuck). Buck likes me white as a ghost.

Your loving alabaster daughter who loves fucking black men.

Signed Brandy the Babysitter

Brandy sat at the kitchen table. The trees outside had already shed their leaves. Buck raked the yard and tarp covered their pool. Her nudist camp brochure showed nice indoor pools. People walked about doing all sorts of fun activities, like painting their bodies with flowers, eastern yin-yang signs, blocks and lines. Some of the guys and girls had fake swimsuits painted on their bodies. The paint was all safe for human skin. They sang songs. They played pool. They walked on water inside this huge plastic ball filled with air. Brandy didn't think she was a candidate for the walking on water. Even their women participated in these quiet times, where they cooked, painted each other's nails, or did each other's hair. All the girls' skin showed a fading summer tan. Most were as white as she was. This kinda shocked her.

In the summer, they went boating, played volleyball outdoors, and jumped on trampolines. The young nudist participated in beauty contests, archery, and limbo contest. Their beautiful beach made Brandy want to move south. She didn't think Buck would move south, though. Best they might do is become snow birders.

She flipped the catalog. The member fees did not set them back. Only reasons Buck would object is that occasionally they took pictures. She decided to call them. "Hello. I'd like to join your nudist colony."

The woman who answered the phone sounded nice and told Brandy she, too, was eight months pregnant. "Pregnant women can join."

"Those rates are really reasonable. I thought, looking at all the activities, this resort might be super expensive."

"No. We can put you up in your own cabin, at Shore Bluff."

"That would be nice. Give us a good view."

"The best view would be the B cabins by the swim pools, during the summer months."

"And it's fall and winter now."

"You'll have to come inside, to our swimming area, or recreation areas, now."

"What happens if your partner, or husband, is a little nudist shy?"

"He can wear a towel until he feels comfortable."

"We're an interracial couple."

"We have no mixed races, yet." She paused on the other line to ask someone else. Brandy heard them talking about the members from Brazil. "Yes, our members from Brazil are black. They are our sister nudist colony."

"They viewed black men before... my husband... he's huge."

The naked pregnant woman at the other end, on the office line, said, "Penis size doesn't matter. Nudism is not about sex. We don't have orgies. We celebrate being born nude and being unashamed of our sexuality. You'll find nudism camp to be less sexual than a fetish sex party will, where everyone outdoes one another wearing skimpy clothes. Nudism is pure."

"That's really beautiful." Brandy almost gasped into the phone. "I'll be sure to tell my husband, nudism isn't about sex. It's about celebrating our natural heritage and beauty."

"So when can we expect you to come down?"

"Uhmmm, next week!"

"I have your credit card number. It's all set, Mrs. Henderson. You'll be in Cabin B, Row #9, all of next week."

Brandy hung up the phone. "I can't believe I signed us up for that. Buck's going to spank my ass, or he's going to celebrate his black skin like never before.

Buck came home with Tawnequa in his arms. "Hello Brandy."

"Hi, Nanny Brandy," Tawnequa said. He let his child lean over and kiss Brandy on the cheek.

"Wonderful, I'm so glad you're here, Buck and Tawnequa." Brandy gave Buck a knowing look. Buck sat Tawnequa down and Brandy took her hand. "Your sister can't wait to meet you."

"She told you that, Nanny Brandy?"

"In so many words, yes." Brandy said, using her softer nanny voice tone. She looked to Buck.

"Buck, we have to tell her how things will be, so she doesn't get jealous, or feel left out."

Buck swept Tawnequa up into his arms. "Honey, let's go shopping and buy your new baby sister a gift."

"Will she get me a gift, too?"

Brandy jumped in, "Pomona's already picked out your gift, last week." Brandy brushed the little girl's corn-rolled hair, "But, she can't let you have it until after she's born."

"Okay. Let's go shopping, Daddy." Buck left with Tawnequa, and Brandy realized she hadn't even told him the good news about Leonard, or the nudist camp. She laughed. Things are getting mighty busy around here.

Brandy went into the children's room and decided where to move the extra bed, so the burgundy crib might better fit. Her own closet had toys for the baby and new toys for Tawnequa. Brandy read a few books about having a new baby around last month, but now, she decided to double her efforts. She wanted the siblings to get along easy, like she and Buck got along. She also remembered the Lamaze class advice, when the child meets the new baby have it in a crib, or bassinette.

After the three of them ate dinner, Buck put Tawnequa to bed. Brandy and Buck went into the living room to talk. "Buck, Leonard Smith agreed to come to the match-making party."

"You... He agreed?" Buck's face showed astonishment. "He knows you're Alice's daughter?"

"Yes. I hope he doesn't think I'm his daughter, though."

"How could he have gotten that idea?"

"All the noise at the airport, engines revving, cargo trucks driving by. The wind noise drowns out almost all sound."

"You said Alice Tuey."

Brandy nodded. "He knows only that I want him to meet someone."

"He guessed its Alice."

"Yes, Buck. He hesitated, though. I hope they left on good enough terms."

"I hope he shows up."

"What if they broke up ten years ago, Buck?"

"Stop that type of thinking."

"I made arrangement for a plane ticket from the Philippines, just in case."

"Cold feet."

"Lover's remorse."

"What if your Mom finds someone over the holidays?"

"I told her to fucking stay single."

"You talk to your Mom like that? Gee!"

"You should hear how she talked to me while growing up. Calling me a white-trash whore."

"She thought you were doing what she liked to do."

"Yep."

"I saw the nudist resort charge."

"You check up on my purchases?"

Buck pulled her toward him. "No

Babysitter Girl. Just remember, it's going to cost a pretty penny to bring our child properly into the world. Not like long ago, when you go into a shed out back and squirt out a child for free."

"Buck, my doctor discourages travel after thirty-five weeks. So, we have to go next week. I'll be thirty-four weeks next week."

"I see. Okay, Babysitter Girl."

"Did the Mexico contract...?"

"Brought in a cool 1 million dollars."

"Why worry about money?"

"Because I want to set up our own Management Consultant Business someday." He leaned over and kissed her deep on the lips. Brandy fell deeper in love with Buck Henderson. She was giddy for him. His passionate kiss showed her he felt the same. Their tongues swirled around. They sucked each other's pink tongues. Brandy rubbed her nose against his wider nostrils, as she turned her face to the other side.

"You're going to make me a partner."

"Not if you keep spending money like its water."

Brandy pulled back, "The place is so beautiful. They even have blacks from Brazil there."

Buck didn't realize that. "I thought only whites became nudists."

Brandy jumped up, "We're going to

become nudist!" She unbuttoned her robe, Buck's blue robe she wore, and swung her heavy tits from side to side.

"I've created a sexual monster," Buck said.

Brandy took a bubble bath and, when she returned, Buck lay fast asleep. He had the nudist colony in his open hand. He also had a hard on.

"Hmmm..." Brandy thought. "I'm going to have to fuck him all weekend to make sure he's drained by the time we arrive. Brandy smiled and rubbed her heavy tits, under her pink towel. She untied the white towel on her head and dried her ash-blonde, short hair. She dropped the towel and admired herself in the mirror. She looked at her tight, flat butt. From the side, she looked like a ship sailing at sea. The curve up, from her Venus mound, took a sixty-degree angle. No centerline ran down her belly. She was pleased her abdominal muscles held together. Her bella-band helped. She didn't want that line going down the middle of her belly, like she saw some women had. She planned to fuck some more and wanted a beautiful, white belly for the black guys to bump against after her pregnancy.

Brandy squeezed her breasts and felt wetness. "I'm getting milk already."

Buck woke up. "Come here, let me take care of that."

"No no, Buck." Brandy laughed. "The baby gets first sucks from this milk. It has nutrients in it."

"What happens if it leaks all over your towel and the bed?"

"That's a waste we can afford."

"Then, I might as well suck some of that spillage before it happens." he said, walking toward her naked body. Buck hugged her and kissed the hollow of her neck and Brandy swooned.

"I'm very sensitive there, Buck." She held his head in place. She grabbed his ass, as he slid his curly, black hair and handsome face down between her breasts. He held his lips there, kissed and sucked her flesh. Then, he moved his head toward her C-cup tits. "I admire how perfectly round your tits are, even as they fill out with milk."

"I always wanted to be bigger than a B."

"I'm satisfied with B or C tits. As long as they are soft," he kissed her breasts near the top of her chest. "White-rosy pink," he kissed the middle of Brandy's breast areolas. "... And creamy to my tongue," he sucked Brandy's nipples and she leaned her head back and sighed audibly. Buck ran his hands down the sides of her body and paused at her belly. "I'm so proud of you, Brandy, for carrying our baby. I can't be happier."

"Does that mean you don't want to suck

my other milky tit?"

Buck kissed her belly button, rose back up, and pulled the heavy, dark red nipple towards his mouth. He slipped her tit into his warm mouth, as if it was a Hershey Kisses candy, and sucked and groped his wife, until her tit orgasms rocked her body. Then, Buck guided her to the bed. He sat her down. He dropped his black pajama pants. He had taken a bath earlier. "All those white nudist girls, bouncing on the trampolines and painting each other's bodies made me horny."

"I'm your wife, Buck." Brandy sat down. Her hands went up, to fondle his black, heavy balls and his blood filled cock. "Let me take care of your needs, while I serve my own mouth-watering ones."

Brandy opened her mouth. Buck guided his hot prick inside her lips. She licked and kissed his dick as it slowly entered her mouth. Then, Brandy did what Buck had wanted for his birthday gift. She knew he wanted to fuck her mouth. She refused to say anything. Her salvia built up in the back of her throat. She adored the underside of his soft penis skin. His corona. From her sex book, given by Heidi, Brandy knew how to do this. She reached down under, behind his balls and before his asshole. This is that sensitive place. She pressed a couple of times and Buck's hot prick jumped in her warm wet mouth.

She loved the fullness and magnificent feel of him in her oral cavity. She pulled his dick out and let it cool off, as she wiped it on her cheeks and in the dimple of her chin. She'd look particularly slutty doing this, the book said. It'd show her man, she really loved his cock. Brandy slowly guided his dark black manhood back inside her mouth and held the cock head tightly between her lips and refused to let him enter. Buck took this as a challenge. He grabbed the back of her ash-blonde hair and pushed. Brandy held her mouth tight. He knew she could suck him whole. So, he playfully pulled her head toward the base of his black candy bar cock. Then, he eased back and pushed forward. "I'm going to fuck this mouth. It's so good." Buck began to fuck her mouth faster and faster. His powerful hands held Brandy's head firmly in place. Brandy relaxed her throat and opened her mouth. She felt her salvia glide all over the top and underside of his black dick. For the first time, instead of looking up into Buck's eyes longingly and submissively, she looked at his black fuck tool as it pierced the white, soft pink flesh of her lips. She marveled at how strong he was. The slickness of his black skin. He hardly had any hair on his dick. Her cheeks sucked in and she waited, as Buck forcefully brought her nose down to his curly, black-hair groin.

She smelled his Brute soap on his dick and loved the manly smell. Her eyes took in the stretching of his skin, as she held tight. He pulled his cock back, only to bang her wet, pink mouth, again.

Brandy wanted to suck in his balls, to show her natural feelings for sucking cock. Buck was having none of that. He moaned and Brandy braced herself as she felt her gag reflect coming. Relax, relax she ordered herself. Let him enter you and have his joy. Take joy in the sharing of skin friction on skin. She flattened her tongue, allowing his cock to ride over it, like someone surfing down a slide. As his cockhead dipped pass her gag reflex, Brandy swallowed, so no drool came out. Buck stared down, at his young, white wife and couldn't believe she handled him. His hands around her hair, entangled, as he pulled her back and forward down on his manhood. He felt masterful and dominate. He could not hold back any longer, he grunted loudly, "Arrrhhhhhhhhhhhhhhhhhh." And let his seed spurt down her pink throat, as he held her head close to his black lower belly.

Brandy kept pushing that soft spot behind his balls, until Buck stop shooting his gallons of wads.

He slowly pulled back, and drool slipped from Brandy's widening mouth, onto the white towel she had dropped below.

"I've never shot off so much cum in all my life!"

"You fucked my mouth soooo good, Buck!"

"What did you do to me?"

"Just a little something a little birdie taught me to do."

"Heidi."

"No, a book Heidi gave me for my maternity gift."

"I like Heidi more and more every week," Buck replied.

"Don't like her too much," Brandy wiped her mouth with her hand and rose up. She rose on her tiptoes and kissed Buck on the lips. "I'm setting her up with Akbar."

"Akbar and Heidi." He laughed. "I've got to see this."

"At the match-making party, you'll see."

"I can't wait."

9 BRANDY'S SEX TAPE

Brandy and Buck walked into the Nudist Colony Office. Three nude white women stood in the lounge talking and laughing, as they walked in. Buck's eyes immediately tried to avoid soaking up their beautiful, nearly pale, skin. One woman looked his age. Another looked five years older than Brandy and the third was their teenage daughter. From their snippet of conversations, Brandy and Buck overheard that they arrived a few days earlier. They wanted to know how the teenage beauty contest worked.

Brandy was guided her husband by his strong black hands to the hotel clerk, a buxom woman with huge DD tits. "We have reservations for Cabin B #9."

"Oh yes, you're the Hendersons. Clarrise told me about you." The lady turned around and grabbed their key. She handed it to Brandy. "The B Cabins are around the hallway, to your left." Her huge DD tits almost dragged on the counter. Her large nipples almost turned Buck on.

Brandy laughed, "Buck, stop ogling her tits."

"You'll find a little looking is okay." Then Clarrise said, "Eventually, you'll find nudism makes all the gawking and staring obsolete." She handed Brandy their keys and turned to Buck. "It's clothes that make the human body erotic, not nudity."

"I can control him," Brandy countered, dragging him away to their cabin.

"Whew. I needed that towel, right then."

"The only towel you need is me." Brandy said, unlocking their cabin door.

"I thought you said clothing was optional?"

Brandy sat her small carry bag down on the queen-sized bed. "You wanted it to be clothing optional."

"You mean..."

"Nude. Totally, Buck." Brandy pulled him down on the bed and sat there, holding their intimate moment. "Help me out of these clothes."

From Brandy's point of view, Buck wanted to see his wife nude. He left her sitting, after he took off her black and pink tube top, and long, floral black and green skirt. She wore open toe flats and black crotchless pantyhose. He took every opportunity to touch her feet and legs. As she contemplated her husband's loving attention, she realized he wanted her black pantyhose to stay on.

"Lay back, Brandy."

"Oh, you want to satisfy my lust first"

"I want to drown your pussy lips with my tongue."

"That's sounds hot."

Buck rubbed her legs up and down several times, making Brandy's temperature rise. Her breasts rose and fell, as she waited for him. His fingers rang, like droplets of water, along her inner thighs and calves. He caught her gaze, as he lowered his black face in between her white pantyhose-covered thighs. His lips kissed her inner thighs, left, then right, and moved closer to her treasure. Her pussy lips seemed like a ripe peach. Her cunt wasn't bald like before. Brandy didn't want to shave too much while in the late stages of her pregnancy. The fact that Buck didn't mind munching on her blonde, hairy muff drove Brandy to a fever pitch. She took charge of her tits' pleasure and began to pinch her large nipples. She laid her hands on her belly and Buck removed them and held them by her sides. Brandy felt helpless and vulnerable to the onslaught of his oral manipulations. Over her huge white belly, a perfect full moon drummed up erotic and loving feelings for her husband, Buck Henderson. Behind that full moon, his big black lips tried and succeeded in raising the tidal waves of her lust. Buck felt Brandy grab his hands in return. He knew she gave in to his passion. He let his tongue trail all the way around her pussy crotch.

Her pussy visibly pulsated in a few minutes. Her clit came out to play. Buck's tongue thrashed about, from side to side, and Brandy's hips began thrusting outward and inward. He slowed her thrusting and flapping legs down by kissing her white thighs, slower and slower. She boldly humped Buck's black face, when he sped up his licking her pussy. He made her wet cavity divulge itself of her liquids... all over his face. Buck let go of her hands to hold her thighs down, to better eat her snatch, again. She reached down and forced his head closer to her tongue, deeper into her cunt. She grew tired of his petty licks. "Stick that long, wicked tongue up my crack slit!" Buck scooped his hands under her flat, white ass and held her there, like a watermelon, and stuck his slippery tongue good up her cooze. She thrashed about, wild, like a cowgirl bucking a bronco horse. "Ride that pussy!" she yelled. Buck held her ass for dear life. Brandy's thighs pressed against his ears, and she knew he couldn't hear anything in the room now. The tightness between the V of her crotch and Buck's head, as his large hands, pulling her tush apart, made her scream out her first cum. "I'm cummmmming, Buck!"

Buck kept licking, probing, and using his large, black lips to caress the inner lips of her slot cave. He wanted to grab her large, smooth, white mama tits, but had to wait until Brandy opened her legs and released him.

His hard tongue flicked her clit button, and it reverberated the movement. Soon, Brandy released her second orgasm. Her hot love juices rolled onto Buck's agile mouth and brown lips. She didn't see why two orgasms were enough. Her body went stiff, and she shifted her ash-blonde head from side to side, as another orgasm crashed down, upon her thirty-four-week pregnant body. Buck lapped at the women's essence flowing out of her pussy, as Brandy squirted for the second time in her life. Buck's tongue explored the deeper and hotter recesses of her folds, and pussy hole, shaking in tiny tremors of ecstasy. Until Brandy screamed, "Buck! You're a wonderful pussy licker! Hmmmmmmmmmmmm!"

Then, Brandy released his head from her leg hold and crashed back down on the bed, exhausted. Buck gave her some finishing licks to taste her purse juices, then crawled up beside her and lay down.

"Buck," Brandy panted, "That was the best oral sex!"

"I can improve, too."

She panted and tried to catch her breath. They lay there and cuddled, hugged, and kissed for two hours. Then, they fell asleep in each other's arms.

After fucking, before having their morning shower and breakfast, Brandy and Buck started getting dressed and both burst out laughing.

"We can just walk out the door nude," Buck said and laughed.

"I know, it feels wonderfully weird and strange."

They held hands and walked out of their cabin, to the community's entertainment center. When they entered the hall, they heard everyone playing in the pool; a bare few sat watching television in a small area. A large crowd gathered, body painting one another.

"I want you to feel comfortable," a man said. He introduced himself. "If you're comfortable being nude, you'll have a good time." He pointed to people body painting.

"We are having a body-painting contest. Anyone can join in."

"Oh, Buck let's join."

"All right."

They went over to an empty spot, next to a mother and daughter team. Buck had something clear in mind for his wife's porcelain white body. On her belly, he painted Monet's water lilies hanging over their bed. On her left tit, he painted a huge sun, but he was careful not to paint her nipples or aureoles. On her left tit, he painted a cloud. Brandy painted a huge fire around his crotch and upper thighs. She put vertical streaks of white, wiggly line paint going up, past his pectoral muscles, towards his chin. She lined yellow arching curves beside the white lines. Then she painted six-pack lines on his abs.

"You trying to tell me something, painting those abs?"

"Not unless you feel like interpreting something." Brandy added playfully. "I'm just having fun. I haven't thought about my Mom at all." She painted some black lines down his thighs. "This is the first time I haven't felt a need to justify my enjoyment of your beautiful black body, Buck."

"We're married now, Brandy."

"I know... It's silly."

"Your Mom likes sex. All Moms do."

Brandy giggled like a little girl. For the first time, she felt totally relaxed. Buck was right; she didn't have to justify liking black men. Or liking sex. All Moms liked sex, or they wouldn't have had children. "Buck," she remembered the couple next to them and whispered. "I want to really fuck a black guy. Not asleep, but awake."

"I was wondering when you'd ask, Babysitter Girl."

"At the match-making party. I want to have consensual, non-emotional sex, like you had with Heidi. The Hot Chocolate Boys of Summer will be there. Heidi and her fourteen other girlfriends and your five black college buddies."

"Ten."

"I can handle ten black men. Can you handle fourteen gorgeous white women?"

He watched her intense blue eyes as she painted on his shoulders, red strawberries and berries.

"A competition."

"Challenge."

"And when your Mom comes into the den, living room, or bedroom?"

"I just keep on fucking like before."

"My bad ass white girl."

"Bitch girl."

The man running the competition carried an air of authority. His long white beard and black round glasses gave off that he might be a judge of contest and game shows in real life. "Gather around. We're announcing the winner of the body paint contest for this morning."

Buck positioned Brandy and her big white belly in front of his hard-on. "I need reassurance, Babysitter Girl."

"Oh Buck," Brandy glanced around and down past her belly. "You naughty, naughty."

"And the winner..." announced the contestant head, "Is Brandy and Buck Henderson." Thirty contestants and their wives, sisters, brothers, and children of all ages clapped for them. "Come forward and let's get the ribbon around you two."

Brandy stepped forward, but Buck held her shoulders. "Brandy, you can't do this to me."

She whispered, back, "Buck, you're not even all the way hard yet." She giggled and broke away.

Buck's black cock dangled between his black legs, a good six inches. On his face, Brandy saw he was concentrating and trying to control his length. She waddled up to the bearded white man in black glasses.

"Oopps... We may need..." as he struggled to put the taupe silk ribbon around her left shoulder, then her belly. The crowd started giggling. "The Henderson's are new to Shore Bluff Nudist Colony. Make them feel welcome."

"We've never had a real black here before," said a young teenage girl to her forty-something Mom.

"That's not true, Cassandra. The Brazilians are black."

"Tan, Mom. Very, very tanned."

Buck folded his hands over his growing crotch. He saw this as an opportunity. "Let me help you with that ribbon." Buck jogged up to her.

"Be careful not to slip on the wet paint," said a white female, about Brandy's age.

Buck quickly stepped behind Brandy. The relief on his face came off like confidence to the crowd of anonymous nudist.

"There!" The contestant head started clapping, holding his small, black and silver, microphone in his hand. "Let's give them a hand. Monet Water Lilies on her pregnant belly made a brilliant canvas."

"We have the painting over our bedroom headboard."

"Oooooohhh," said the contestant head. "They brought their bedroom to Shore Bluff." He laughed.

The wife, who had sagging great tan tits and a scar along her belly, said, "You bring the bedroom with you to the nudist camp every day, Harold." She laughed. "Leave the couple alone. In fact, it's quite time for us women and girls..." She pulled Brandy's arm, while a man with a camera tried to position his lens. "Us girls and women need to get this paint off you right away. To the showers." Several women and their daughters followed the older woman, and Brandy, to the showers, where she quickly removed the paint. "This paint is safe for human skin. Nevertheless, we don't want to take any chances. Babies, at your stage, might be very sensitive." After removing the paint, the woman whisked Brandy away to a small living room. They sat her on a couch and all fluttered around her huge belly.

"Is it a girl, or a boy?" She handed Brandy her taupe ribbon.

This woman took a hairbrush off a table and began to lovingly brush Brandy's hair.

"Girl."

Cassandra, the young teenage daughter, lifted Brandy's feet onto a cushion. "Any names, yet?"

She began to open a bottle of polish remover.

"Pomona. Oh, a pedicure. I have been so busy."

"You can't even see your feet, now." All the females laughed.

A tall woman sat down and took a small bag of cotton balls. She placed them between Brandy's toes. Ah, an Asian Pacific name."

"I'm kinda of ticklish on my feet."

Cassandra said, "Probably a Philippine

name."

A young college student took her fingers and began swabbing them, removing her old nail polish. "Actually, I do know some from the Philippines."

The office desk lady came into the living room. "I see the women have made you very comfortable."

"Is he related?"

"He's a friend of my Mom's."

"Not your father, with your chalk-white skin."

"Her skin is so beautiful."

"You received a phone call from an Alice Tuey, it was forwarded here from your residence."

Brandy, who was reclining on the couch, sat upright. "My Mom called."

"She left a message. "I will be there for the match-making party."

Brandy left the three-hour quiet time with the women more beautiful than before. They braided her hair. Her toenails and finger nails they colored hot pink. She wore a little mascara and make up on her young white skin. "The natural roses on your cheeks, lovely," one elderly lady complimented.

Buck had a good time, too, talking with the men. They chatted about business, soccer championships in EU, and made some business contacts as well. When Brandy came out from the hallway, Buck's eyes bulged wide.

"Buck! Buck!" she waddled in her winner regalia and new hairdo. "Mom called and left a message. She's coming to the match-making party!"

"What did they do to you, Brandy? You're gorgeous." He held her at arm's length and admired her hair. Brandy held out her manicured fingers and lifted one foot, showing her pedicure.

"Hot pink!" He nodded and smiled. "You women really took great care of my wife. I appreciate it very much." He started walking with Brandy back to their cabin.

"We have to go home and prepare Buck." Brandy said, walking like a penguin, as Buck held her around her huge waist.

"I've made some good business contacts, too."

"See," Brandy slapped his flaccid black dick. "You two behaved yourself as well."

"There is nothing erotic about business talk."

"Ut unnn," Brandy put her right arm around Buck's black hard waist. "When you talk business to me, my pussy flutters every time."

Buck and Brandy got home a day

earlier than planned. This gave them an entire day to plan the matchmaking party. They bought new cushions and pillows, blankets, condoms, and lubricants. They purchased another five new black on white porno tapes. That's when Brandy realized... she never saw their original tape. She had on her pink maternity dress, black stockings, and white gym shoes. He had on brown dress pants, a checkered blue and white lumber shirt, and loafers.

"Buck, where is the hidden camera?" Brandy said, surveying the room from her office desk.

"You really want to know."

"You didn't make it!"

"Yes, I did. Do you want to watch it now, or in front of everyone, at the match-making party?"

"You'd play it at the..."

"I planned on slipping it on the table of porno tapes." Buck's eyes looked delightfully wicked to her. He narrowed his eyes and smirked. "Up to you."

"I want to see it!"

"We're too busy, now."

"No we're not."

"Exhibitionist slut."

"Your white exhibitionist slut, Buck."

"That you are. Wait a second."

He came back with a DVD and popped it into their small DVD player in the bedroom, inside the mirrored chest a drawers. The DVD was wired to a large 55-inch flat screen, behind the water lily painting.

"You sneaky, perv!" Brandy shouted and slapped his ass, as he carefully pulled Monet's painting down and placed it on the floor. The flat screen blinked, and then turned on.

"There is no sound, Brandy."

"No sound."

He laughed, and pulled her close to him. "We need to sit at the foot of the bed."

"Ahhhh! Buck, this is uncomfortable."

"I agree. Only if you're not fucking while watching the tape is it uncomfortable." He pointed to the upper right and left corners of their bedroom. "I placed two small cameras there."

"Two."

"I had no clue how you might lay, away or towards the door."

Brandy lay on her side and Buck spooned himself behind her flat, sexy-wide prego hips. The screen came on and showed Brandy waiting and waiting, pleasing and touching herself.

"I look like such a slut, lying there, begging to be fucked."

"This is one of my best scenes. You don't often find out how your woman touches herself, when she's completely alone." He reached down and tried to touch Brandy's clit. She slapped his hand away.

"Not yet. I want to see this." Brandy's sex flush flowed all over her white face and breasts, as she realized how naked and white she seemed. She held Buck's hand tight.

Buck grew stiff. He placed Brandy's hand on his crotched, but she snatched it away.

"I was three months pregnant and I look so fat."

"You do not look fat."

"What will I look like now?"

"You'll look beautifully pregnant, Brandy."

"Oh, is this after all the fucking, or before? I'm so wet!"

"Before."

"I really needed a cock up my puss. Look at all the juice flowing down my ass crack and buttocks."

"Like I said, this is some of the best scenes." Buck slowed down the remote for a second and zoomed in on her breasts. "See how you're touching your nipples, so light."

"Buck, no one was coming in the bedroom. I was going lust crazy."

"I have these bookmarked."

"Turn to Akbar!"

Buck flicked the remote buttons and

Akbar walked into the room. Brandy and Buck burst out laughing. Akbar was so full of beer he walked right past her naked, sperm-drenched pussy and ass, into their bathroom.

Brandy didn't want to reveal how much she wanted him and his deep voice fucking her. Akbar seemed so dominate out there, amongst the boys.

"Here he comes, Brandy."

"I saw him. My eyes were not closed." Brandy realized her pussy gaped open almost inviting him. Her legs lay across the bed, her feet facing the door. Of all Buck's black college buddies, she wanted to fuck Akbar consciously, not faking. Now, she was practically nine months pregnant, and she didn't want to hurt the baby. Brandy laughed. Her eyes stayed transfixed on the screen. "Did you see the look on his face? He knows he's getting sloppy thirds!"

"There is nothing sloppy about your sweet pussy, Brandy the Babysitter."

"Right there..." Brandy couldn't help tossing her hands up, and caressing both her breasts in a reflective desire. Then, she dropped both hands by her sides. "I thought he knew I wasn't sleeping."

Buck laughed. "He had to make believe it was true, too. Those were the rules of this game. They listened.

Akbar said, "I'm going to hit this white

pussy, too."

"Buck his nine-inch cock nearly killed me."

"Surely you're joking."

"A girl's pussy has to adjust. And if she can't see fully, what she's adjusting to, it makes it really exciting." Brandy watched Akbar's nine inches of live dick and his huge cap across the top. "I wanted to do him doggy style, but I couldn't say so. I just kept saying it in my mind, Buck. 'Doggy style, Akbar. Doggy style.'"

Buck replied, "I wondered why he was so confused. Open delicious, white pussy and he didn't even know what to do with it."

Akbar said, "Fucking cover girl, nice round face, look at that sexy dimple in her chin." He grabbed Brandy's legs, then said, "Fuck this!" He twisted her legs, causing Brandy to make a "Gumph," sound. Then, he pulled Brandy back onto his hip. She lay limp, waiting.

Buck laughed. "Now there I thought the game was up. How can you twist a woman's legs around like that and she not wake up?"

"It still took him years to get me into position. I wanted to rise up on my hands and knees and say fuck me with that nine-inch cock."

"This was funny, too. He couldn't easily fuck you, Babysitter Girl."

Akbar squatted lower. Placing his boner at the mouth of her sex, in just an inch, Brandy rolled her hips upward and he slipped out. Akbar tried again. He squatted, placed his sex at her lips, and pulled her back on him, about three inches. Then, he lifted her hips up higher and pushed her body forward, so that Brandy now rested on her left shoulder. Brandy made a moan sound and placed her elbows crossed, under her face, while Akbar achieved his desire.

"I had to watch, Buck."

"His cock went in a long time."

"You can see me sighing, trying to encourage him secretly.

Brandy sighed. Six inches.

Brandy sighed. Seven inches,

Brandy sighed. Eight inches.

Brandy tried to sigh, but grunted.

Nine inches, Brandy said, "Oohhh, that's good. Fuck me, fuck me, fuck . . ." and let her voice trail off.

Brandy and Buck found her statement hilarious.

"You talk in your sleep, fuck in your sleep." Akbar said.

Brandy shrugged her shoulders. Anything is possible in a sexual fantasy.

Akbar figured she did sleep like a stone. He pounded Brandy's pussy for a good three minutes before releasing his progenitors into her white pussy gash, to go ova hunting. He pulled out and watched her clutching white, wet snatch, puckering so hard, Brandy's asshole moved visibly in and out, in and out.

"Even your asshole wanted to get fucked."

"I was a lust-filled whore that night."

They laughed at the end, when Akbar ran and picked up his pants and left.

"That's enough Buck," cooed Brandy. I want you to fuck me doggy style, right now. That film makes me want to fuck you most of all, honey. I can't believe we made this."

"It's great, Brandy."

10 BRANDY'S MATCH-MAKER PARTY

In the dining, kitchen, living, den, powder, and bedrooms, a big heart-shaped red balloon floated on a string, displaying the rules in white lettering. Wear a symbol 1, if you don't want to offend your mate symbolizes this is an "oral only orgy" for you. Wear a symbol 2, if you and your mate agree you can totally fuck around. Have fun all. 3, always look for the symbol number on the person you want to fuck.

Brandy walked around in her favorite pink nightie held together by five white bow ties. On her left thigh, a big black Roman numeral I. On her right thigh, a big pink Roman numeral II. Music blasted throughout the house, a mixture of rap,

R&B, and rock, but the music undulated going from low to medium volume, and this gave the matchmaker party a surreal air. Brandy suggested to Buck that she didn't want people sitting around, like at Heidi's maternity party. Music and a clear set of rules should stop all that. Nearly everyone had already shown up including Heidi's girls, Amelina, Christiana, Eliza, Elizaveta, Gyszel, Hanna-Maria, Hely, Leela, Margery, Margit, Quela, Sibbe, Upritsa, and Zaahira. Buck's college buddies strutted around naked, Hagen, Rex, Akabar, and Suhuba. Not to be outdone, the Hot Chocolate Boys of Summer all wore black bow ties and both numbers painted on their thighs. Buck wore symbol 2. He held a drink in his hand, as he talked to Hagen in the dining room, "Nice technique, pushing Brandy's legs together. She really liked that."

Hagen's nimble quick fingers played inside Gyszel's pussy as she stood there, hanging on him, wearing a symbol 2 on her breast. Her knees buckled once, then twice, as her climax approached. "Buck man, you saved my life letting me fuck Brandy. Now, when the MILF teachers toss me their panties during our parent-teacher talks, I know exactly what to do."

They laughed and Buck looked around. He saw Akbar and Heidi chatting softly, over in the corner recliner. She sat on his lap. Buck did a double take. She sat directly on his lap. His nine inches of black meat stuffed comfortably up her coochie snorcher. Heidi's big bubble butts lifted the symbol one on her left ass cheek and the symbol two on her right ass cheek, when walking. Heidi laughed and lowered her head to Akbar, occasionally, and fed her right firm, golden D-cup tit to Akbar, teasing him. Then, slowly putting it to his lips and withdrawing her boob delight. He wore a smile, and for once, his voice held to a whisper. Brandy mentioned Heidi could handle Akbar and that seemed to be the case.

Everyone moved around. Brandy kept track by going from room to room, seeing who was in there and who was fucking whom. The voyeuristic thrill of officially keeping track of her guest's happiness made excitement ripple through her full prego body.

Amelina trouped around sizing up Hagen, Rex, Akbar, and Suhuba. She wanted to hold the two largest phalluses in her hand. That would be Akbar and Luke. Heidi had Akbar busy all night and Amelina hated to wait. Amelina went up to Akbar and Heidi, and said, "Can I hold his black barber pole?"

"Don't you need a partner dick to get off on your fetish?'

Amelina held Akbar's nine-inch cock,

slick with Heidi's fuck juices. "Hey Luke, get your big dick ass over here," Amelina yelled.

Luke had Hanna-Maria on her back. Her knees showing symbols 1 and 2 on her kneecaps, pressed to her boob flesh. Luke complained, but came over, and Amelina got her fantasy. "I'm holding two of the biggest fucking cocks ever." She got on her knees, kissed Akbar's slick dickhead, and licked Luke's dry, stiff, black cock. Her facial expression of ecstasy and happiness eased the frustration of Heidi and Ferdina alike.

"Can I go Mistress, Amelina?" Luke begged.

"Go. Fuck Hanna-Maria's brains out." Amelina ordered. "Rise Heidi." Amelina took Akbar's cock head and guided it back into Heidi's warm, moist, pussy sheath.

Walking into the dining room, Brandy's hand lay on Suhuba's naked shoulder, making him feel like a man. "I'm glad you were my first and darkest, black cock, outside my marriage."

"You saw me."

"We filmed everything."

"No. Shit." Suhuba looked around in the dining room. He shouted to Buck, "I heard you turned me into a porn star, Buck buddy!"

"You turned yourself into a porn star, Suhuba."

"Hagen, Akbar, Buck filmed us fucking his wife, months ago!"

"Ahhh man," Akbar said shocked.

"I have to see it," Hagen said, raising his voice and keeping his fucking rhythm going.

Heidi said, "Brandy, you wench. You made it seem like you'd never fucked outside your marriage! Whore!"

"Bitch! I fucked them inside my marriage." Brandy laughed. "We planned everything."

"I want to tap that sweet pussy of yours again," Suhuba whispered.

"Then let's go into the living room." Suhuba guided Brandy by the hand into the living room. Buck and Brandy had removed nearly all furniture people could not fuck on. Upon entering, they viewed Hely practicing her acrobatics, laid over their living room brown couch, her backwards again, as Rex's brown legs straddled her face and she sucked down his sword like a real pro. Margit danced on the low coffee table in her summer-cropped college T-shirt that said, "Bad Girls Fuck for Fun!" She went bottomless and her body almost distracted Brandy. "Hey bad girl, come on over here and suck my tits, while Suhuba fucks me silly."

Margit stepped down from the table like a real stripper pro and sauntered over to Suhuba and knelt down. She slurped his black cock into her mouth, before Brandy's protests laughter.

"Warm him up for me, Margit."

"That's what I'm doing," she said, in between slurps of Suhuba's hard, lean cock. Margit rose off her knees and Suhuba's dick pointed toward the recliner. Brandy followed and knelt over it. Her waste high enough, so her belly rested firmly on the chair. She looked back and her ash-blonde braids trembled, as she made her ass dance, preventing Suhuba from finding his mark. Margit laughed.

"Don't worry," Suhuba said, "You're next."

"No she isn't," said Ray. He pulled Margit down to the carpet and raised her legs up on his shoulders and started fucking her like crazy.

Brandy has passed by as Margery had Skylar pinned down on his back in the dining room area eating her pussy.

When Brandy finished fucking Suhuba, she went through the other rooms to check on her guest. In their kitchen, Eliza and Zaahira in a sixty-nine ate each other on the blue air mattress-covered sheet, while Suhuba parted Zaahira's pussy lips and slipped his dark cock down her hungry pussy slot. Each woman had a half-eaten banana stuffed into each other's moist cunt. Tall Hanna-Marie, leaning up against their refrigerator, wrapped her leg around Tate as he pumped hard and fast into her pussy. Brandy thought they were going to make yogurt out of the milk from all their shaking-fucking pleasure. She shrugged and said, "That's the cost of having fun." When white women and black men got together, all lust broke loose.

In the kitchen, ninety-eight-pound Mylle tried putting Rex's beer can wide dick stuffer into her small pussy stocking. She squealed and moaned. She hopped up and down as Rex sat on the burlap wrapped stools and let her bounce her petite ass cheeks on his black hard thighs. That beer can of a hot prick didn't seem to be making any progress. Brandy said, "You want some KY to get that pussy splitter inside you?"

"No," Mylle said defiantly.

"How did you get my barber pole up your snatch, Brandy?'

"I fucked three other men first." She winked. "And I loved every minute of fucking them before you."

"You loved my cock."

"I sure did, and if Mylle doesn't wear you out, I'm going to fuck you, again. Rex, the wine bottle."

Mylle and Rex laughed. He wasn't that wide.

Mylle got an idea. She put her breasts on the cold granite kitchen table, so her pussy channel opened wider, and Rex slipped in. She lay back into Rex's arms and pulled his head towards hers. Then, kissed him on the lips. "Good things come in small packages."

"You got that right, Mylle," Rex replied.

Brandy ventured on, to the bedroom, because the locked bathroom door spewed out pleasant moans and cries of "More dick and less talk, Wick." That must be the emotional black-haired Christiana and Wick, Brandy giggled.

In their bedroom, Brandy watched the commanding Luke, on his hands and knees, in their bed, eating Sibbe's pussy, while Uprisita lay under him with her legs looped over his buttocks. Her ass touched his ass, Luke's cock deep inside her quivering cum. Brandy almost got dizzy trying to figure out how Upritsa figured out how to entangle themselves. Brandy held a goblet of wine in her hand. She smiled and couldn't believe how well this was going. She figured two or three match-ups already pointed toward the marriage altar. She hadn't heard a word from her Mom, yet, though. Nor did Leonard communicate anymore. All she knew was some happy soul cashed the ticket to the USA and used it on the flight. Leonard, indeed, behaved a bit mysterious. Brandy walked round and talked to everyone.

Ferdina dragged Hagen into the bedroom, fell to the floor, and forced his dick down her hot steam box. Her legs splayed wide, waiting. The bare cunt opening and closing like a mouth trying to gobble something up. When she heard Buck grunting, "Open that ass wider," she hurried in to see Leela's ass up and rolling, accepting his huge cock past her "ring of fire." Brandy ran up and slapped Buck's ass hard. "Put some emotion into that fuck Mister!"

Buck turned and grabbed her wrists. "Help Leela, come massage her tits."

To his surprise, Brandy had no problems getting down on her knees and rolling Leela's small tits in her moist palms. Leela kept ducking her head between her legs to see Buck's black balls banging her white ass cheeks. Brandy touched them both all over. She loved the feel of their slick, sweat-soaked skin. She loved the smell of their bodies merging. She even knelt down and raised Leela up. The two women rubbed and their breasts flesh kissed. Her small boobs against Brandy's mama milky tits.

Margery, Quela, and Zaahira lay on their backs as Tate, Hagen, and Ray lay across the girls and three drenched pussies made sopping sounds in unison.

Whatever clothes the three women and men wore, long since disappeared.

So much fucking happened everywhere that Brandy wished she had a camera. Then, she remembered, Buck had the hidden cameras in the bedroom. All she had to do was direct everyone to fuck in the bedroom. She made an announcement. "All fucking to be done in the bedroom for the time being. I have an unexpected guest arriving."

When everyone gathered and began fucking in the bedroom, Buck whispered, "What's up, Babysitter Girl?"

"I want to film this!"

"Good idea."

"Besides, I don't want to scare Leonard and Mom away." Brandy checked her watch. "It's about that time for their arrival."

In the powder room, Skylar and Ray double penetrated the Asian-eyed Quela. Ray fucked her pussy standing in front of her. Skylar fucked her asshole from behind. Quela's eyes rolled into the back of her head. Her symbols of 1 and 2, on each shoulder, disappeared in the blackness of their thrusting chest and heaving hips.

Heidi and Akbar now fucked doggy style. Before going to the bedroom, Buck decided to take Leela in the bedroom bathroom and fuck her face. "I love for men to fuck my face," Leela cooed. "I have a wide open mouth and no gag complex."

"My kind of woman to fuck," replied Buck.

"I get to sit on your face in return, black Buck." She said, as his huge hands grabbed the back of her head.

Leela spread her knees wide, on the small bathroom carpet, and relaxed her throat. Buck pulled her forward, then backward. His dry black cock quickly became slick with her salvia. He pulled her mouth forward, again, then back, and his entire cock shinned black, like new leather. Brandy walked by and saw some girl getting her face fucked. Brandy didn't realize it was her husband, Buck. She had just sat on Luke's face. Her fist pumped fast and furious, until Luke's big cock spurted his white volcanic sperm high into the air. Her pregnant belly secure on his chest. Her cunt smothering his face. His only device to lick Brandy so well, she moved around and squirmed on his expert tongue.

In a few minutes, the doorbell rang. Brandy opened it. "Mom!"

Alice wore a black cashmere coat over her little black dress with spaghetti straps. Her high heels had one strap.

"Brandy!"

They hugged and tears flowed in their eyes.

"Mom, you look hot." Her Mom wore some highlights in her dark hair. Her blue eyes had smoky eyeliner. Her cheeks blushed with subtle roses. "Look at you. I don't know," Brandy said, walking around her Mom. "You might steal away my black husband, Buck."

"I'd like to meet Buck. But, why all the nude people and the place decorated like this?"

"Mom. We're having a matchmaker party. An orgy. Fifteen white girls and ten black guys."

Just then, Quela came out of the bedroom giggling. She rushed back into the bathroom and tried to close the door. Naked Tate came following her with his huge slick, black prick bobbing up and down.

Brandy shrugged her shoulders. "I have a surprise for you."

"Surely, it's not to fuck one of your black men friends."

"It's Leonard."

"Leonard!"

"He's in a cab now on his way." The cab horn blew. "That's him, Mom." Brandy raised her hands up to shush her. "Don't say a word."

Brandy waited until he reached the door. Out the peephole, Brandy saw a black man in a pilot's uniform walk towards the house. He rang the doorbell and Brandy opened it.

"Excuse my dress, Leonard. We're having a black men and white women's match-maker party," Brandy laughed.

"You can't be more than eighteen!"

"I'm eighteen and married to Buck Henderson."

"You're Alice's daughter."

"Yes. Come in Leonard."

He hesitated.

"I assure you all is okay."

"I can't stay long."

Brandy brought Leonard into the living room and stood there.

"Leonard!" Alice said in a tearful voice.

"Alice!" They moved toward one another slow and cautious. "I've missed you so much, Alice."

"I missed you, too. Leonard." She hugged him and they hugged with tears in their eyes for almost five minutes. Brandy just watched.

"Now Mom, there is no need to hate black men anymore."

Alice cried softy. "I never hated black men."

Brandy wiped her Mom's tears. Alice's make-up started to smear.

"I hated missing Leonard." She paused. "I am sorry, Brandy. I know I lashed out. I wanted to prevent you from having the same heartache I endured for nineteen years."

"We were so young, Alice." Leonard apologized. "I had no job. You could not leave with me for two years."

"I didn't know what to do either..."

"There was nothing we could do, Leonard." She pulled his hand to the brown leather couch.

He sat down and they held hands and talked quietly. "I waited... I tried to come back."

"My Mom was still alive. I... I was still confused and John hadn't left, yet."

"Brandy told me you're single."

Alice cast a why did you say that look? "I'm still married, but John ran off. I'll get a divorce." She sobbed. "Leonard, I've always loved you!"

"Aww baby, I knew it. I knew it!" Leonard turned to Brandy. "I want to thank you for persisting in getting us together." He paused. "I didn't know what to think."

"Me, too. She told me, Leonard, it was for her baby shower."

Brandy, again, shrugged her shoulder, loving their surprise faces. They wanted to fuck. Brandy just knew it. "You two haven't had each other in a long time." She pulled the wine bottle out of the ice bucket and poured some in a goblet. "Cheers to the Happy Reunion Fucking!"

Leonard chuckled, "Has your daughter always been this naughty."

"You really messed Mom up, Leonard. She hated all black men and accused me of doing every black boy, during my middle school years." She took a sip of wine. "That's why I'm so fucking hot for black cock now."

"You should have seen her letters to me," Alice shook her head. "Her speech is mild stuff, Leonard."

"But I am right," Brandy drained her glass. "You two now want to fuck."

"Why not, Alice?" Leonard kissed Alice gently.

"It's been such a long time."

Alice raised her little black dress over her head.

"Why Mom, no panties or bra!"

Leonard shook his head, "You look so ravishingly beautiful."

"You used those words long ago, Leonard."

"Those words ring true today as well." He reached out to feel her breasts. She reached out and took off his pilot jacket. As he groped her nipples and bare ass, Leonard lost his shirt to Alice's fast fingers. She bared his hairy chest. He shook his pilot jacket and white shirt off his body. He rose and Alice deftly removed the belt buckle, and had his pants around his knees. She leaned back and stared at his black cock. Admiring it.

He removed his pants. "Your white skin

is so luminescent. She glows in the dark. Doesn't she, Brandy?"

"Buck called me his light bulb in the dark."

Alice ran her hand down her black, airplane strip of pussy hair over her alabaster clit. "I'm ready Leonard. Let's catch up where we left off."

Leonard's nine-inch cock reached his length, all the way out, to Brandy's surprise.

"He is fucking huge, Mom."

She locked her legs around Leonard's back. "Give me everything you've got, Leonard."

Leonard leaned into Alice and plunged his hot poker all the way down her pussy gap, in one swoop, as Alice tossed back her head. She moved her black hair out of her eyes. "Fuck me good, Leonard."

Leonard raised her legs around his black hips. "Let's get married after this, Alice?"

"Yes, Yes Leonard." She sighed, as his nut sacks began softly bouncing against her pussy lips.

"Let's not delay."

"I know a friendly judge who works on the weekends." Brandy cooed, watching them screwing and twisting their limbs around each other.

"We'll do it tomorrow, Leonard." Alice cried, "Now, just fuck the empty space out of my deep cunt palace."

"I have the tool to do the job, Alice."

Brandy clapped and called Buck. "Buck!" Buck ran out and saw the two strangers fucking, like in a woman's porno tape. "Buck, meet my Mom, who loves black dick again, and Leonard, her soon-to-be black husband tomorrow."

"Congratulations Leonard and Alice." Buck Henderson hugged his wife's wide waistline. "You two brought Brandy, the Babysitter, into my arms... Thank you."

"Yes, thank you... "Brandy slumped down and Buck caught her.

"You okay, Babysitter Girl!"

"Oh Buck, it hurts. I'm not due for a week yet and it hurts..."

Buck yelled, "Call a doctor!"

Leonard pulled his black cock out of Alice, quickly.

Alice said, "Brandy, put your legs up on the couch." Brandy's Mom swung Brandy's right leg high on the back of the brown leather couch. "Brandy, I... I know we haven't been..."

"Mom! Buck," Brandy tried to point to her cell phone on the kitchen table. "Call Doctor Kappel. My speed dial!"

"Brandy, darling," Alice said, on her knees before her daughter, "I'm going to be a certified nurse next month."

Brandy closed her eyes, because of the pain, "How? Really Mom... Why didn't you... Oooooohhhhhh!"

Everyone came out of the bedroom, naked and sweaty, from fun sex.

Margit reached her first. "Brandy, I wish I was further along in my nursing course."

"It's okay, Margit."

Leonard remained quiet.

"Stand back everyone, give Brandy room to breathe," Alice said in a surprisingly commanding voice. She replied softer to Brandy, "I wanted you to make up your own career mind."

"Who is she?" someone asked.

"You never dressed like a... Mom!"

"I'm sorry for keeping so many secrets, Brandy," she looked at Leonard. "Secrets from you, too."

Brandy clutched her clinching stomach. Then, her water broke over the couch.

Buck said, "I'll get some towels."

"Someone go into the kitchen and get some hot water."

"Will Doctor Kappel make it here in time?" Brandy said, in pain.

"I don't know," Buck said, returning with the towels.

"You can do this, Brandy," Alice said. "I never made it to the hospital when you were born."

Brandy closed her eyes and suppressed a scream. "Uggggg, I think she's coming!"

"I can see the head," said Sibbe.

Heidi wiped the sweat away from

Brandy's brow. "You're going to be all right, Brandy. If you can take a big, black cock, you can certainly deliver a baby."

Everyone laughed.

Alice felt slightly embarrassed. She rushed about and positioned Brandy's knees to her heavy milk-filled breasts.

Buck said, "Doctor Kappel's on his way, Brandy."

Brandy heaved and let out a loud scream. Then, a soft cry filled the room, as Leela, Hagen, Luke, Ray, Upritsa, Amelina, Elizaveta, and Zaahira held hands. Rex, Akabar, Asian Quela, Suhuba, Gyszel, Tate, Margery, Wick, Mylle, Hanna-Maria, Eliza, Skylar, Hely, and Ferdina held their breaths. Emotional, teary-eyed Christiana cried, "It's so beautiful. I've never seen a live birth!"

"It's a girl," said Leela.

Alice had the baby girl, in a fresh towel, all swaddled up and warm. "Brandy, here's your baby girl."

"Congratulations, big man," complimented Luke.

"Thank you, Luke."

"And I wondered if you were fucking your wife any," said Hagen trying to make the situation lighter. People laughed.

"Pick out a name yet?" one of the girls asked.

"Pomona," said Brandy quiet, simply smiling and staring at her new daughter.

Pomona's brown eyes looked around, as if trying to take in all the strange faces.

Alice busied herself, pulling out the placenta, and cleaned up Brandy.

A car screeched in the driveway. Their doorbell rang and Doctor Kappel rushed in with his medical bag.

"Is everything all right, Brandy!" he said.

"I'm starting a nudist colony, Dr. Kappel, you're overdressed." Everyone laughed. "See. Dr. Kappel, this here is my Mom," Brandy looked at her Mom. "She's a registered nurse. She delivered Pomona."

"I've heard so many wonderful things about you, Mrs. Tuey."

"Well, that's kind of an exaggeration, Doctor." Alice deferred, "I made her comfortable and cleaned her up. Mother nature did the rest."

"Well, Brandy," Doctor Kappel said, "you always were healthy."

"In more ways than one," said Brandy, as she let out a laugh.

"Oh, we all know what that means," said Akbar in his deep voice.

Everyone laughed.

"Buck, you going to hire Leonard into your new Management Consultant Firm?"

"I think we can work something out, Brandy."

Leonard moved over and shook Bucks hand, vigorously. "I want to come back to the states and work." He reached out to Alice, standing next to Christiana. "Alice and I want to get married and have a child of our own."

"Oh no, you don't," said Brandy, "I'm too old to be babysitting a younger sister!"

"You're going to be all right, Brandy." Doctor Kappel said, "Mrs. Tuey, you did a wonderful job delivering her. A fine job."

"See Mom, we have a wonderful mixed family after all."

"Yes, darling, we do."

"And Buck, I'm the last babysitter you're ever going to hire!"

"You're the only babysitter I need, Babysitter Girl."

—THE END—

AUTHOR'S NOTE

Readers: I want to expand a few of the stories to see where the characters can be explored further. If there are any of the stories that you would like to read more about again, I'd love to hear from you!

Visit my blog at www.ericresher.com

Join my newsletter for free exclusive previews
http://www.ericresher.com/in

Follow me on Twitter at
http://www.twitter.com/ericresher

Like my page on Facebook at
http://www.facebook.com/ericresher

Discover my books at major ebook retailers everywhere.

www.ingramcontent.com/pod-product-compliance
Lightning Source LLC
Chambersburg PA
CBHW020114180626
46812CB00006B/2600